The Spitfire Project

Hayley McLennan

Copyright © 2013 Hayley McLennan

All rights reserved.

ISBN-10: 1482306476
ISBN-13: 978-1482306477

Alice,

You showed some interest when I was writing this, so here is the final product!
Thank you for being supportive and for always being there for me.
I love you,
H xxx

For Madi.

With all my love, always.

CHAPTER ONE

We have finally reached London. I swear the journey from Paris has never taken so long. There was a strong headwind, and the days seemed to stretch out because I knew that time was of the essence. I have rifled through every paper in this study and found no clue as to why Lady Austin's life would be in danger, but if I have to trust Father completely, then that is what I will do. I am still not sleeping, whenever I close my eyes I see him die all over again. I have always known that working on airships is unsafe, and we have fought off pirates in the past, but I still expected Father to reach old age, although I had no reason to. I always hoped to take over captaincy of the Spitfire after his death – or even if he decided he would rather spend all his time tinkering with his inventions – but only now do I realise how difficult it will be.

Of course, it is made no easier by my promise that I would 'save Sola Austin', despite not knowing from who or for that matter, why I have had to lay off all crew I do not trust utterly, and I am not looking forward to taking to the skies again without them. I know I can rely on Henry, Gloria and Ethan for anything, and I believe I trust Tristan Lynch, James Riddle, and Rob MacKinnon, as they have been with us for so long. I will have to, anyway. To try and man the ship with any fewer would be madness.

Britain is in turmoil at the moment too. I have just been reading in the paper about the postal strike – the latest in a long line of worker uprisings. I support the motivation, but I must admit I like to get my post.

Nevertheless, it has been nice to see Marcus again, possibly the one upside to this stop in London. I wish I could persuade him to come with me, but I know trying would be futile. He has so much to do here. I hate the danger he puts himself in by housing such people, never mind the work he does for runaway slaves, but every time we have this argument he reminds me that Father helped him when he was in that position. What can I possibly say to that?

"See this is why I hate staying on board," came a low voice from the doorway. "You always run away to do something in the mornings."

Laughing, Mac put down her pen and closed the logbook before he could see what she had written.

"I'm pretty busy, Marcus."

He placed his hands on her shoulders, gently massaging them. "I know, *Captain Sheridan*, but if you would stay in my rooms, I'd at least be able to trap you for a few more hours."

"I prefer not to visit your guesthouse," she replied snidely. "I don't like your clientele."

"It's hardly as if they would do anything to hurt you."

"It's more a matter of principle. Besides they haven't exactly treated you wonderfully."

"That's my business, Mac.," he said, exasperated and still clearly refusing to discuss it. "I don't understand you. You hate the aristocracy and what they've done, the anarchists want to overthrow them, but you hate them too. Is there anyone you actually like?"

Mac stood and smiled up at her best friend and occasional lover. Rising onto her toes, she pressed a soft kiss against his lips.

"I like you," she said, smiling. "Coffee?"

"Yes please," he sighed, shrugging his shoulders in defeat.

"Relax then, I'll just get some from the galley."

Mac couldn't help tensing again as she descended the spiral staircase to the lower level of the Spitfire. Being around Marcus relaxed her, it always had, but the instant she was away from his company she remembered why she was stressed. If dealing with her father dying in her arms and taking over control of his airship hadn't been bad enough, there was his last request to consider. As he choked up blood, he hadn't attempted any goodbyes. His words were desperate, urgent - *"This is no pirate attack. It was planned. Sola Austin is in danger. Save her. Promise me you'll save her."* - it was the echo in her head that had forced her onwards for three weeks back from mainland Europe, despite harsh weather and technical problems. But now that she had reached London, the enormity of actually kidnapping an aristocrat was hitting her. What the hell was she thinking? Well, that much was obvious. She had promised her father.

"So," opened Marcus, as Mac re-entered the study with two mugs of coffee. "Is there a reason you've moved in here?"

All her belongings had moved from her bedroom into her father's study. Her study. There was even a blanket and pillow up on the mezzanine. Of course he had noticed.

"It's the best place to work, and all I'm doing is working at the moment. It's convenient."

Fixing her with an I-know-better stare, Marcus said, "Mac, it's just across the hall from your bedroom, which has been stripped. What the hell is going on?"

Mac sighed, and placed the mugs down on a small round table, which she sat at, indicating he should take the seat opposite.

"I may not be back in London for a while, Marcus."

"Is that really a while? Or is that... ever?"

"A while, I hope. I have something to do. It's important. I promised Father I would. But it could be dangerous."

"This dangerous something involves having someone on your ship who'll need a bedroom?"

Mac couldn't help chuckling. "You're far too clever for your own good, Marcus."

"Most white people seem to think so."

She sipped her coffee. There was no reply to that. If his skin colour were different Marcus could easily be a successful businessman or really anything he wanted. But then, if his skin colour were different, if he hadn't had the experience of slavery, of running away, would he still be Marcus? And if he didn't devote his life to helping other Negroes when they needed it most, would she still have the same enormous respect for him?

He took a swig from his mug and stood.

"You know I'd love to stay," he said by way of apology, placing a hand over hers.

She stared at their hands together. Her skin was weathered and browned by the sun, but still it looked shockingly pale in comparison to his. Then he distracted her by using his other hand to tip up her chin, and gently kissing her.

"Be careful."

Mac nodded and squeezed his hand before releasing it. "You too."

When she heard the door close behind her, she also got to her feet, and took her coffee out a door in the corner of a room, onto a small private balcony that stretched across the back of her ship.

Leaning onto the railing, she slowly drank her coffee as she looked out over the city of London, wondering what in the world she was about to get herself into.

One thing Mac loved about being docked in the city – one of the only things – was that she largely had the Spitfire to herself. People had family to visit or shopping to do, or they simply wanted a few days off. For many of them, the ship was work. For her, it was home.

The only other person aboard was Ethan Carlisle. A young and brilliant inventor, she kept him around not because he was a great airman, but because he was a genius. She had given him the workshop on the lower floor, which her father had used for his work. It was an oddly shaped room, curving around the front of the ship, but Ethan was already intimately familiar with it, having been Patrick Sheridan's protégé. Now it was totally his. He'd even strung a hammock up at the very front, and Mac was sure he'd stopped sleeping in the crew quarters altogether.

It was boredom and anticipation that caused her to drift over to the workshop after she'd washed out the mugs. She chapped lightly on the door, partly out of courtesy, but largely because she had no idea what he was working on and if her entering would ruin his concentration at a crucial, and possibly explosive, moment.

"Come on in."

As she'd expected, Ethan was at a worktable, bent closely over some clockwork parts with a magnifying glass flipped over the left lens of his goggles – they too, had once belonged to her father, and seeing Ethan in his room with his things was disconcerting. Yet another reason to avoid this ridiculous part of the ship.

"Am I interrupting important work?"

It took a few seconds for what she'd said to register, and when it did he snapped straight up, shoving his goggles up onto his head, which pushed his chin length black hair out of his face.

"Nothing that can't wait, Captain," he said, with an easy smile. "Do you need me?"

The crew seemed to have gotten used to calling her 'captain' far faster than she had gotten used to hearing it.

"No, I just wanted to check you're good to come with me tonight."

He frowned. "What? Actually into the house do you mean?"

"Yes. Is there a problem?"

"Just that someone else might be better suited... Henry, or Tristan?"

"I'm not comfortable with this either, Ethan," she said steadily, reading his reluctance as fear and doubt, both of which she shared. "But I need Henry and Tristan on other things. I want you with me, if only because you're the only one who really knows how to use those gadgets of yours."

"Oh. Alright then, I suppose."

The mention of gadgets had set him onto more comfortable territory, as it was supposed to. Ethan had never been relaxed around her. By the time he joined the crew, she was already practically running the ship, and he took her as an authority figure. Now she actually was one, it might not be such a bad thing.

"Thanks, Carlisle. I appreciate it. Anyway, I'll leave you to your tinkering."

With so little else to do, Mac went back up to her study to read, although she knew she should really be dealing with accounts. The strange spiral of anticipation, stress, boredom and grief that gripped her was going to make today even more unbearable than every other day since her father had died. But by tomorrow, they would either have Sola Austin or they would not. And there was something to be said for even that level of certainty.

CHAPTER TWO

I don't want to go to down to dinner tonight. Being back in Town after a month in the country house is making me nervous. I know that I must meet with Jesse soon but I have no idea how to speak to him. I haven't seen him since that night. But all of that is in the back of my mind right now. At the moment I am just terrified to go to Duke Bernard's house.. I have thought and thought, but I still have no good explanation for why I was rifling through his papers. The look of horror on his face when he caught me has barely left my mind – only when I have been thinking of Jesse, or wondering about that file .

It wasn't even anything that could be useful to the anarchists. I was looking for bank records, for letters to other government officials, for evidence of corruption... not engineering diagrams, of all things! I wouldn't understand them if I had time to read them properly, never mind the brief glimpse I got. But there is still the matter of my father's name in the footnote – the words 'George Austin', which drew my eye in the first place.

Maybe it is a good thing that Duke Bernard has invited us again. Maybe he has forgiven me for what I shall just have to call aimless curiosity. And – though I hate myself for thinking this – maybe it will give me the chance to find out more. All this time with Jesse and his friends really has changed me.

Anyway, I must get ready now. There will be plenty time for pointless musings later, I'm sure.

Sola sighed and looked up at the mirror, eyeing her reflection critically. Leading a double life between aristocracy and anarchism had started to take its toll. There were dark shadows under her eyes on her otherwise pale skin, and her long blonde hair had begun to hang lifelessly. If her friends saw her like this, they would think she was ill. She would be able to fix it with some time, and make up. But first she needed a bath. Travelling all day was exhausting.

Almost a year before, Sola had met Jesse Armitage at a party. It was the kind of gathering frequently thrown by the younger members of the aristocracy when their parents were absent – full of illicit substances and behaviour. She enjoyed them enough, though the facade of rebellion they enacted became repetitive.

But at this one, there was someone new. An enigmatic man in his early twenties, a few years older than the other guests. He drifted around the room, seemingly aimlessly, but Sola would later discover there was a definite purpose to his actions, to who he spoke to, and what he said. He extracted information skillfully, making his sifting for knowledge seem like idle gossip – a talent that she liked to think she had picked up, if not quite to the same degree.

They spoke for an hour that night, and she was still unsure whether he had been manipulating her, or if he genuinely enjoyed her company. She, however, had definitely enjoyed his. Somewhere in the conversation, he let slip just a little of his mask, and spoke passionately about social issues, about politics, about issues she was aware of, but from an angle she had never considered. She was entranced. He must have seen the potential then. At the end of the night, when she opened her bag to write in her journal, there had been a napkin tucked inside the front cover, with an address written on it in bleeding black ink.

The guesthouse was in a part of London she had never, never been to, nor ever wanted to. She knew it was from him though, and the thrills that sent through her were not entirely from the dangers of going to such a dangerous area alone. Maybe she should have forgotten about it. Maybe she never should have gone. But she did.

Unaccompanied, in her plainest clothes, Sola had turned up at the door, and when she knocked gently, it was opened almost immediately by a tall Negro man, with dark stubble over his head and chin.

He took one look at her, and shook his head.

"Friend of Jesse's?"

The voice was surprisingly warm and pleasant, but she had frozen in fear and could only nod. He pretended not to notice, standing aside to let her in.

"They're upstairs."

They? That had been the first clue that something more complex than she realised was going on. She nervously made her way onto the first floor, and walked into a small dingy room full of people, with Jesse standing at the front, speaking to them all. It didn't take long to work out this was a meeting of anarchists. There were people of all ages, Negroes and Jews, men and women, all just staring at Jesse while he spoke. And it wasn't hard to see why. Sola was soon gripped by his rhetoric, seduced by the image of equality and empowerment than he wove.

After the meeting he had pulled her aside to explain how useful she could be, given her position in the aristocracy.

"I took a risk," he said, "bringing you here. A lot of people disagree with me. They think you'll betray us. But I know you're clever, Sola, and I know you understand there is a problem in this twisted society. Will you help us to fix it?"

It was like being put into a trance. A trance that she still went into when Jesse was around. There was something alluring about him, and even more than that, about working for a cause. The thrill of teasing knowledge from her friends to pass on, of sneaking around houses at balls and dinner parties to try and find something useful. She wasn't sure how much she had actually done, but she was convinced that she hadn't been useless. Until she got caught by Duke Bernard, anyway. She freaked and ran to the guesthouse, into Jesse's arms, and the next thing she knew they were kissing and then – she blushed remembering it. It had been her first time.

Now she was just back from a summer in the countryside and Duke Bernard was inviting them – Sola and her aunt, Lady Judith Austin – to dinner again. Sola had begged Judith to say they were too tired, to say anything, but true to form, her guardian had been unhelpful, saying it would be rude, and that she should behave properly for god's sake.

Sola put the finishing touches to her hair and make-up before donning a dark purple dress, with a black pattern and bustle. She looked like she was going to a dinner party, but felt like she was going to war. The Duke could have forgotten the whole incident, but it seemed unlikely. Frankly, Sola had no idea what to expect.

CHAPTER THREE

This whole thing is a ridiculously idiotic idea. I don't want Lady Austin aboard my ship, making such an effort to get her here is stupid. And also, if we're caught, which we will be, I'll probably hang. Brilliant. Thanks, Father.

I get the feeling that I'm not hitting an appropriately formal tone for a captain's log – I should probably treat this a little less like a diary.

Finalised trade deals this afternoon and stocked the hold – transporting cotton to a factory near Bristol next week.

Also organised tonight's venture. Henry will take charge of the ship, and fly it to somewhere over the Austin house, where he will hang down a ladder. I can already see this being awkward. Ethan and I are about to head over to instigate our part of the proceedings, that is, kidnapping the bloody girl. I keep trying to think of it as saving her, but that doesn't help much.

Mac read back over the entry and couldn't help laughing at herself and the odd situation she had been put in. She couldn't show any uncertainty in front of the crew: the only thing that kept them willing to do this was unwavering loyalty to her father. They had heard his words as clearly as she had. *Promise me.* She sank her head into her hands, gently massaging her temple.

"This is no time to have a breakdown, Mackenzie," she whispered, and taking a deep breath, gathered herself.

The rest of the crew were in the lounge, playing cards.

"Hope you're staying sober, Ethan," she said as she opened the door. "It's nearly time."

"Yes, Captain," he said promptly.

Looking at him, Mac saw that although he looked determined, he had gone faintly green. She walked over to the cabinet.

"On second thoughts, Carlisle, maybe you need a drink."

"I'm fi..." he trailed off as he saw she'd pulled out two glass tumblers and a good bottle of whiskey. "You're probably right, Captain."

Mac laughed, pouring a single shot into each glass. She raised hers to the room.

"Thank you for agreeing to be part of this. It truly is a testament to your courage and loyalty. Good luck, everyone."

"Good luck," they echoed back to her, and she downed the glass.

"Bottom's up, Carlisle. Time to go."

With the poor security in the houses of the aristocracy, Mac wondered why the anarchists hadn't sneaked in through the servants' door and killed the lot. A coin in the hand of an underpaid scullery maid would be enough in most situations, however she knew that they couldn't be seen. When the news that Lady Sola Austin had been kidnapped broke, even a slightly dishonest maid would probably crack and go to the police. Their plan was even simpler – walk up to the door, and go in.

Doing their best to blend in, Mac and Ethan approached a deep blue double door. Praying that she'd gotten the right address, Mac nodded. Ethan drew a small silver device from his pocket and clicked it over the lock. There was the faint burr of tiny gears turning for a few seconds, then a smooth click, confirming it was done. He slipped the gadget back into his pocket, and courteously opened the door.

Mac couldn't help but smile. The way Ethan's mind rose to any challenge never ceased to amaze her. The house was large and grand, and they soon came upon the immediate problem of having no idea where Sola Austin would be.

On Mac's lead, they began to climb the first set of stairs they came across. She hoped Ethan wasn't assuming she knew what she was doing. A young black servant – *or slave,* Mac thought bitterly – emerged from one of the rooms. She straightened her back.

The Spitfire Project

"We're looking for Lady Sola Austin's room?" she said, trying to sound as authoritative as possible.

The woman regarded them with suspicion. "Why?"

Shit.

"We're the heating engineers," she heard Ethan say behind her. "We were told there was a radiator fault in the room."

The maid still didn't look entirely convinced, but she nodded. "The last room in this corridor. But I think Lady Austin is still dressing, so please wait until she's gone out for the evening."

"Of course."

When the maid had left, Mac laughed. "Heating engineers! Ethan, I bloody love you."

He forced a smile. "That was the easy bit."

The information that Austin was still in her room was an added bonus, which almost countered her annoyance at the maid seeing them. Mac pulled out a chloroform-soaked rag that she had tucked into her utility belt – it had probably helped with the engineer story, now she thought about it.

"Ready for the difficult bit?" she asked with a grimace.

"As I'll ever be."

Mac turned the handle and quietly opened the door. Lady Austin was at a vanity table on the other side of the room, putting in earrings, and Mac knew she didn't have long before Austin noticed her in the mirror.

All the same, she walked as softly as she could, and made it to a few steps away before the other woman began to turn.

"What the he-?"

She sprinted the last metre and shoved the rag over Austin's nose and mouth. The aristocrat struggled, flailing and managing to scratch Mac's neck and face, but she kept the chloroform held close, and eventually Sola Austin passed out in her arms.

Wincing, Mac laid the body gently on the floor.

"Are you hurt, Captain?"

"Nothing fatal," she said, feeling an irrational rush of fury as a scratch on her cheek stung. "Grab some of her stuff and shove it in a bag. Clothes, shoes, toiletries. I've got to signal the Spitfire."

There was a tiny balconette outside the room, and she stepped out onto it. She took another chemical soaked rag and wrapped it around the iron railing, then set it alight.

"That will definitely burn out, not burn the house down, right?"

Ethan glanced over. "Yes, it'll be fine."

"If you're sure. Do you have a bag together?"

He lifted it to show her

"Then we wait."

It didn't take much time but it felt like an eternity as they sat there, terrified that someone would open the door at any second. Mac didn't realise she was holding her breath until she saw the rope ladder drop down onto the balconette, pooling on the floor, and exhaled in relief.

Within a few seconds, Tristan had clambered down it.

"Where is she then?"

Mac tilted her head towards the centre of the room, where Ethan had laid the unconscious Lady Austin on the bed. Tristan strode over, and effortlessly picked her up, tossing her over his shoulder.

"Are you going to be okay getting her on board?" Mac asked, looking at the ship, which suddenly seemed a long way up.

Tristan grinned easily. "Do you doubt me, Cap?" he asked.

She laughed and shook her head.

Tristan was built to work on airships – he was wiry and ridiculously strong. Most crew could scale rigging with some ease, but she had never seen anyone navigate the ropes with the grace of Tristan, who moved as though he had been born climbing. Still, she couldn't help but be nervous as he began to climb, and stared at the limp body over his shoulder until they disappeared into the night sky.

The rope shook to signal that he had reached the Spitfire.

"You first," Mac said to Ethan. "Let me take the bag, just focus on getting up."

She tried for an encouraging smile, but he just grimaced in reply, his lips fixed together in determination as he reached out and gripped the ladder, placing a foot on the first wrung. Again Mac watched, terrified that he would lose his focus and fall, or freeze up completely. Maybe putting him in this situation had been a mistake. If a year working on an airship hadn't been enough to cure his phobia, would anything be able to? The doubts joined all the others that had taken up residence in her mind.

He took a little longer than Tristan had, but the ladder eventually shook. Pride flooded Mac. No one could say the man wasn't brave.

Still smiling, she began to climb.

CHAPTER FOUR

Today has been the strangest day of my whole life, and I have had some pretty strange days. I don't remember much from last night, just glimpsing someone in my mirror and turning around, and then the next thing I knew, I woke up, not in my bed, not in my room... not even in London.

Sola rubbed her eyes and stared around the strange room with growing confusion and horror. It was large, with a double bed that she had woken in, a vanity table, a desk, and a screen with a wardrobe behind it. The windows were circular, and she wandered across to one of them, then recoiled.

Instead of seeing other buildings or even a landscape, she was looking out across sky and clouds. She was on an airship.

She tried to make sense of it, but drew a blank. Looking down, she saw that she was still wearing the dress she had put on the night before, but was sure she'd never made it to Duke Bernard's house. She remembered wishing for something to get her out of the dinner invite, but she hadn't expected this.

On a rug at the foot of the bed was a black bag, open to display some of her clothes, with her journal sitting on top. She picked it up, running her hand over the patterned brown leather. She'd been chronicling her thoughts for years, which usually helped her to make sense of things, but she doubted it would now.

Instead, he focused on the small things. Her dress was crumpled, and at any rate, it was far too big to travel in. She may as well change. Selecting a relatively simple blue dress from the bag, she didn't bother to go behind the screen since no one was around. After changing and fixing her hair as best she could without a brush, Sola felt she had stalled enough. The only way to find out what was going on was to leave the room. Half of her hoped that the door would be locked as she reached for it, but it swung open, revealing a corridor lined with doors on either side, with a spiral staircase at the far end. She walked slowly, trying to make no sound, although she wasn't sure why. Anticipation rose into a familiar sick feeling in her stomach, which she had felt many times before when sneaking around houses for Jesse.

Manage your nerves, she told herself, as Jesse had said to her in the past.

The staircase led both up and down, but Sola knew that the lower levels were likely to be little more than an engine room and a galley, so she chose to ascend. At the top of the stairs was a door, and when she opened it, she stepped out onto the deck.

A man with dark skin and very short hair was hanging off the rigging, seemingly oblivious to the drop below him, casually talking to another man who was leaning over the railing.

"Have you bloody fixed it yet?" asked the second man, who was pale, with red hair and a beard.

"Give me a break, I'm not Ethan," replied the other. "Do something useful, would you, MacKinnon?"

"We'd have Ethan do it if he wasn't so fucking scared," MacKinnon retorted. "You may climb like a monkey but you're probably about as clever as one too."

"Fuck off."

"Language," Sola heard someone behind her say, and turned to see a third man, stocky and strong-jawed with long blonde hair. "There's a lady on the deck."

The other two men turned around instantly.

"James Riddle," said the blonde man, stretching out his hand.

Shocked into courtesy, Sola went to shake it, but the instant her hand was in his, he bowed down and pressed his lips to it.

"Give it a rest, Riddle," said the redheaded man in a thick Scottish accent, laughing at the expression on Sola's face. "Robert MacKinnon, call me Rob. It's a pleasure to meet you, Lady Austin." He also stretched out his hand, and then added. "I promise I'll only shake it."

The final man swung up onto the deck – and Sola could see Rob's point, he did move a little like a monkey.

"Tristan Lynch," he said with a smile. "How are you feeling, Lady Austin?"

Manage your nerves.

"Confused," she said honestly, "and irate, to put it mildly. Where's the captain of this ship, I want to speak with him."

Her brisk tone didn't achieve the desired effect. All the men looked as though they were on the verge of laughter.

"Top deck, by the wheel" said James. "Follow me."

He led her a short flight of steps to a smaller deck at the back of the ship, where three more people were speaking to each other.

"Lady Austin wants to speak to the captain," he said, still with an edge of laughter to his voice.

The person nearest to them turned – a young woman, barely older than Sola herself, and a few inches shorter, with tanned skin, an angular face, and dark brown hair pulled into a bun at the nape of her neck, though parts had been tugged loose by the breeze.

"Yes?"

"I said I want to speak to the captain," Sola reiterated, looking behind her at a broad, bearded man who was chuckling gently, and the older woman by his side.

But her reply came again from the young woman.

"Then *speak*, Lady Austin."

"You're not..." she trailed off, looking at the faces of those around her and being unable to detect any joke.

"I assure you I am. Captain Mackenzie Sheridan of the Spitfire, at your service. If you would prefer to speak with Henry, then I'm more than happy to pass on the privilege of your conversation, but if you want to talk to the captain, then you're just going to have to get over your shock, Lady Austin." With that, she turned away again, and said to the other woman, "Gloria, could you fetch Ethan for me?"

With a sympathetic grimace as she passed Sola, Gloria walked down the stairs and disappeared through the door to the lower floors.

"You're going to dump this on Carlisle?" said James, undisguised glee in his voice.

"I could change my mind easily if you're not careful, Riddle," warned Captain Sheridan. "Do some bloody work, would you?"

"Yes, Captain," he said enthusiastically and smiled broadly at Sola again, before running down to join Rob and Tristan, taking the steps two at a time.

"So how does someone become an airship captain so young?" asked Sola, trying to sound curious rather than accusatory.

"Their predecessor dies too soon," replied Captain Sheridan, not looking back at her. She pulled a compass from under her shirt, and flicked it open.

After studying it for a few seconds, she shut it and tucked it away again. At last, she turned to Sola and looked her in the eye.

"You're very quiet for someone who wanted so desperately to speak with me, Lady Austin."

Sola bristled. "Well then, Captain Sheridan, would you care to tell me why I'm here?"

This provoked a wry smile. "I would if I could," replied the captain.

"Well you kidnapped me!"

"Yes, I did. Believe me, I want you here about as much as you want to be here."

"Then take me back!"

She raised her eyebrows. "Would I really have gone to the effort of taking you if I were just going to drop you home again? Do you think I just decided that you'd like a little day trip, Lady Austin?"

"I don't understand."

"You and me both," the captain mumbled, almost to herself.

Infuriated, Sola was about to try again when Gloria reappeared, with another man by her side. He was tall and pale, with straight black hair that grazed his shoulders, which he brushed out of his eyes when he smiled at her.

"Glad to see you're well, Lady Austin," he said, before turning to Captain Sheridan. "You wanted me, Captain?"

"Did I interrupt anything important?"

He shook his head. "Nothing that can't wait."

"Excellent. Lady Austin, this is Ethan Carlisle. Ethan, take her down to the galley, make sure she's eaten. Then just make sure she's..." Mac shook her head and shrugged, "out of the way. Take her to the workshop if you like, but if she's going to be in your way just take her back to my... *her* room and I don't know, get her a book or something."

"*She* is right here listening to you, you know," Sola said sharply.

The other woman glanced back in her direction. "I realise, I also don't care."

A flash of rage passed through her, and before she even knew what she was doing, Sola swept up her hand to slap Captain Sheridan, who reacted like lightning, catching her wrist and gripping it hard. She didn't let go, or loosen her hand, and after a few seconds it began to hurt.

"I would not recommend it, Lady Austin," she said, stressing every word. "Ethan will take you to get breakfast now."

Sola looked up at the new arrival again.

"Come on," he said. "You must be getting hungry."

Now it had been mentioned, she did feel an ache in her stomach, and so she reluctantly forced down her fury and followed him back inside the ship.

After grabbing something to eat in the galley, which was surprisingly clean, Ethan told Sola she was perfectly welcome in his 'workshop' if she wanted, and though she had no idea what it was, she figured that it would at least be better than being in 'her' room with no company at all.

The workshop was full of strange machines and wooden tables with gears and mechanical parts spread all over them. It was split into two parts as it curved around the bow of the ship, and at the front there was a hammock strung up. Sola could tell that she had lost some of Ethan's attention the instant they were inside the door. He pulled on a pair of goggles with several lenses attached, and flipped one of them down over his left eye, sitting down at a table with tiny metal parts on it. He shuffled them around, picking up the tiniest ones with tweezers, and slowly began to assemble them.

For a few minutes she stood watching, but eventually she lost interest and began to wander at random. On the other half of the room there was a cabinet full of bottles that she would bet that they didn't contain drinks. Ethan's head popped around the corner.

"Be careful with those," he said.

"I wasn't going to touch them," she said defensively. "I was just looking."

He relaxed. "Sorry. You're bored. I just get distracted in here, there's so much to work on."

"Is that why you sleep in here?"

Ethan laughed. "Sometimes I think best at night. The guys don't appreciate being woken if I get inspired at three in the morning and have to stumble down to the lab."

"And Captain Sheridan doesn't mind you being here?"

His brow furrowed. "Of course not."

"She doesn't exactly seem the flexible type."

"She's going through a tough time at the moment. She'll warm up."

Sola laughed harshly. "I don't care if she warms up or not, I care if she lets me *go* or not. I don't see how she kidnaps me and then *she* gets to be pissed off about it!"

"I appreciate Captain Sheridan hasn't exactly explained herself to you," said Ethan, continuing in the same measured, neutral tone.

"There is no excuse for kidnap," Sola said coldly.

Ethan just shrugged. "All the same, I'd give up on hoping she'll let you go any time soon."

"Why?" Sola finally asked, exasperated. "Why am I here? If she wants a ransom she should just say! I came into my inheritance about a month ago, I can get the money."

Looking straight at her, Ethan shook his head.

"We don't want money, Lady Austin," he said seriously. "We want to protect you."

"Protect me from *what?*"

Ethan sank into the nearest chair.

"I honestly don't know. But we were asked to do it by a man I would have given my life for, and I trust him implicitly, even now."

"Even now?"

"He died recently," Ethan said quietly.

Sola instantly made the connection. "The previous captain?"

"Yes. He was truly brilliant. This was his workshop, really, and he taught me so much here – that's why Mac gave it to me after he died."

"Is 'Mac' Captain Sheridan?"

"Now she is, yes. It hasn't even been a month yet."

"But everyone's perfectly happy to take orders from her? Even the older man – Henry?"

Ethan couldn't help laughing. "Yes. Henry's first mate but he has no desire to be captain. And Mac's basically been running this ship for about two years, her father spent most of his time working here. She's young, sure, but she's made for it. More than Patrick was."

"I thought you said he was brilliant?" Sola asked, curious despite herself.

"Oh he was," Ethan's face split into a massive grin. "Single-handedly the best inventor and most ingenious mind I've ever witnessed or heard of. Kind, and wise. I adored him, but he wasn't made to be an airship captain by a long shot. He lived in his head too much – who could blame him? If I had his brain, I'd be content to live in it as well."

"He wasn't a god, Ethan," came a voice from behind them, and Sola span round to see Captain Sheridan standing there, trailing her fingers over one of the worktables.

"Well it sounds like he was a sight better than you," Sola snapped, irritated that just as she had began to find things out, the captain had interrupted.

To her surprise, instead of looking annoyed, Captain Sheridan smiled gently.

"Without a doubt, Lady Austin. But he was still only a man."

"Not to me, Mac," said Ethan.

This time her face split into a wide smile. "No, nor to me. I just came down to tell you I'll have James cover the cooking today."

"... what do I have to do in return for that?"

She glanced meaningfully at Sola.

"You're already doing it. Can I do anything to make your stay more comfortable, Lady Austin?" she asked, managing to be so over-polite that her question sounded rude.

"Some information would be a nice start," replied Sola frostily.

Mac looked down at the work surface she was touching. "My predecessor was also my father," she said, a tiny hint of emotion in her voice for the first time. "His dying request was that I save you – I don't know how or from who or what. That's all I know. So have a think about it, Lady Austin. What have you done to get yourself in such trouble?"

An image of Jesse sprang immediately into her mind, but Sola said nothing. She didn't trust Captain Sheridan, and wasn't about to risk putting Jesse in danger.

"Well?"

"Nothing. I have no idea. I'm not even sure I believe you."

The captain laughed. "You can't seriously think I *want* an arrogant, entitled, aristocratic brat aboard my ship."

"I certainly don't want to *be* here."

"Would you look at that – we do have something in common after all. I'll see you two at dinner."

She span on her heel and walked away.

Sola collapsed into the nearest chair. "Ugh. Should I expect her to drop in often?"

"No, she doesn't usually come down here," Ethan said, looking confused. "I wonder why she didn't just send James to tell me about the cooking."

"Probably wanted another chance to have a go at me," said Sola bitterly. "I'm already a prisoner on her ship, it's not like she doesn't have the upper hand."

"She's..."

Sola raised her eyebrows. "Really, there's an excuse? She's what?"

"...grieving."

"So are you, it doesn't seem to have made you unpleasant."

"Erm, thanks? Look, why don't I get you a book or something..."

Rolling her eyes, Sola gave in and dropped the conversation. "I'll go grab my journal. At least someone thought to bring it."

"That was me."

"You were in my room?"

"Yes."

"Did you read it?"

Ethan looked offended. "Of course not."

"Right. And Captain Sheridan didn't either, right?"

"I don't think she even saw it, Lady Austin."

"You can call me Sola, Ethan," she said, suddenly tired and feeling like she could do with a friend. "I'll be back down in a minute."

CHAPTER FIVE

We are on course for Bristol and making good progress. Lady Austin is as objectionable as I predicted, but Ethan seems to like her well enough and he's keeping her out of my way. I just wish I knew what connection my father had to this girl, why her life was so important to him – important enough to give his for.

I have read over and over every entry in this log, which is illuminating in some ways, as far as learning about Father goes, but sheds no light on the issue at hand.

I miss him so much. I could even cope with Sola Austin's presence if he were here, I think. Short of that, I miss Marcus.

However, there is little use in dwelling on what I can never have. I should make an appearance in the lounge and have a drink with the crew.

Mac wasn't used to the task of recording her thoughts, and still wrote a little uncomfortably. She knew it was meant to be therapeutic, but couldn't help thinking a good sleep would do the trick. Unfortunately it didn't seem like that would be happening in the near future. It wasn't that the mezzanine was uncomfortable, but trying to make sense of the turn her life had taken kept her awake – and if she did drift off, she was plagued by nightmares. She yawned and gently slapped her cheeks a couple of times to wake herself up, laughing when she remembered Lady Austin's earlier attempt to slap her.

At the end of the corridor was a room her father had turned into a crew lounge, with a dining table and two smaller coffee tables, along with various chairs. Gloria, Henry, James, Rob and Tristan were already playing poker. Gloria's pile of chips was by far the largest.

"Do you want to play, Cap?" asked James desperately. "We could start afresh!"

She laughed; the crew always managed to improve her mood.

"Not a chance in hell, Riddle, I'm going to sit here and watch Gloria kick your arse."

True to her word, she opened a bottle of cider and pulled an armchair across to the table.

"How long do you think before we reach Bristol?" asked Rob.

"A few days."

"Someone special you want to see?" teased Henry.

Rob's pale skin blushed easily, and it went pink instantly, causing the whole table to erupt into laughter.

"Speaking of," said James, "I have a bone to pick with Lynch here. He didn't tell me that our Lady Austin was such a looker."

"I was more focused on not dropping her," Tristan said, rolling his eyes. "Not that I think you stand a chance, Riddle. If she were interested in any of the lowlife on this ship, it wouldn't be you."

"Oh, you think she'd want you? English ladies are not interested in, erm, darker men, even if they are half and half."

Tristan easily could have taken offence, but it wasn't in his personality. Mac thought of Marcus and smiled to herself. She was hardly an English lady, she supposed.

"No, I think you might find Lady Austin prefers brains to brawn..."

Mac realised what he was implying, and laughed. "I think Ethan might have more sense than that. Or I certainly hope so."

"He'd have to be mad not to go for it if he had the chance," said James. "Then, I don't think inventor-boy would know what to do with a woman. If one wandered stark naked into that workshop of his, he'd probably try to explain steam distribution to her."

It was a little cruel, but they all laughed, knowing there was some truth in it.

"She's been there all day though," Rob said. "They even ate in there. They must be getting on."

"I'll bet you a pound that Ethan gets the girl," Tristan said with a smirk.

"You're assuming he wants her," Mac said dryly.

At this, there was a lot of snorting and raised eyebrows from the men at the table, and even Gloria mumbled something that sounded like, "Be serious."

She raised her hands in surrender. "Never mind then. Taking the bet, James?"

As the banter continued, Mac thought about it. There was no denying Austin was pretty, possibly even beautiful. She had long blonde hair, bright green eyes, and a soft face that Mac supposed would be pleasant, though she hadn't seen it in anything other than a scowl. If something did happen within the crew it could become awkward. She knew Tristan wouldn't try to pursue her – the thought of all the possible complications would be too off-putting to him, he liked an easy life. James on the other hand, most likely would. His ego wasn't unjustified: he was a good looking man who had plenty success, though Mac wasn't sure if it was just the law of large numbers. She was fairly sure Rob wasn't interested. Not in Sola Austin, and not in, well, women. She wasn't certain, but she'd never ask.

Which left Ethan. He was far from a flirt, but there was something in what Tristan had said about brains. It was intriguing to think of her crew in this way, as by the time she'd met most of them, she was already with Marcus. Their arrangement wasn't exclusive, but she had never met another man she felt measured up.

Suddenly the conversation died, and she was woken from her train of thought by the silence. She instantly saw why. The last two people on the ship had come to join them.

Ethan cleared his throat, trying to dispel the awkwardness. "Um..."

Taking pity, Rob rose to his feet and walked over to the drinks cabinet. "Do you two want anything?"

"Beer, thanks," said Ethan, smiling with pure gratitude at the Scotsman. "Sola?"

She tucked her hair behind her ear. "A glass of wine, if you don't mind?"

"'Course I don't. Pull up a chair, I'll bring them over."

They all shuffled a bit to allow two more chairs to fit in.

"Would you like to play poker?" James asked eagerly.

"Sure," Ethan replied. "Do you play, Sola?"

She shook her head. "I never have, but I wouldn't mind learning."

"Excellent," grinned James.

Mac laughed. "Expertly done, Riddle."

Grinning, Gloria said. "Don't worry, Mac, I'm keeping his money."

"I should hope so. I expect you to beat him this time too."

"Damn straight."

Part of Mac — a large part — wanted to leave the room, but she objected to allowing Austin to drive her away from her own friends on her own ship, so she accepted a hand as Henry began to deal again.

The previous conversation had made her hyper-aware, she couldn't help noticing how closely Ethan and Austin sat, with Ethan looking at her cards and murmuring advice by her ear. He was an exceptional poker player — the type of mind that could understand all those mechanics evidently also understood the complications and patterns of the game. However, he played his own hand without any particular flair, cruising easily while making sure Austin wasn't losing out.

Mac pursed her lips, and glanced around the table. She caught Tristan's eye, and he raised his eyebrows knowingly at her. She tilted her head toward him in recognition, a silent and reluctant 'you might be right'. James glanced at the pair and shook his head in disbelief. Rob lightly punched his arm, laughing. Gloria and Henry were just smirking to themselves, more focused on the game than the others.

The two new arrivals seemed utterly oblivious to the amusement, or at least to the cause of it. After a while, Mac began to relax again, despite Lady Austin's presence. For the first time in a few weeks, she actually felt lucky, as she looked around with a rare sentimentality, knowing that if she couldn't have her father or Marcus around, there was no one she would rather be with than her crew.

It was a late night for them, but Mac didn't mind. By the time she made her way back into the study and climbed up onto the mezzanine it was around one in the morning. Sighing, she grabbed one of the many books that were scattered around the mattress, and lit a candle. There was almost no point in trying to sleep these days. Only when her eyes stung with exhaustion did she blow out the flame and put down the book, and then she lay with them closed, unsure if she was asleep or awake, until the rising sun began to glow through the portholes.

She took the light as a sign that it was acceptable to get up, and was soon down from the mezzanine, relieved to no longer feel as though she *should* be asleep. Usually she would go down to the galley to get coffee in her father's shirt, which she had taken to sleeping in, but with Sola Austin around, she wasn't entirely comfortable. She dressed in breeches, boots, a cream shirt, and lifted her compass from the desk to hang it around her neck. Most captains clipped theirs onto their waistband or belt, but her father had always worn it on a chain.

"Compasses give direction," Patrick said, smiling at his daughter. "And if any part of me needs direction, it is surely my heart."
Privately, the fifteen-year-old Mackenzie thought that his brain, which seemed incapable of focusing on one idea at a time, was more in need of a compass.

Anyway, she chose to wear it over her chest, where her heart would pound against it when it beat hard, just the way he had, in the hope it would give her guidance aside from the geographical. So far, it had not. As a last thought she grabbed her utility belt, with her tools and weaponry, which immediately made her feel more secure, and pulled on a pair of leather fingerless gloves.

She pulled her hair back and twisted it into a long plait and rubbed her eyes. That would have to do for now, she would bath later.

Thankfully, no one else was awake, and so Mac managed to make herself a coffee and take it to the back balcony unnoticed. Here she would be undisturbed until she was ready to deal with running the ship and handling Sola Austin. She watched as the sun emerged, lighting the patchwork of fields below them in a warm orange glow, and tried to imagine living down there. As usual, she couldn't.

Shaking her head she looked up again. Another ship had appeared on the horizon. She rolled her eyes. According to recent trade laws, she had to raise a specific flag when around other ships to prove that they weren't pirates. It was utterly pointless – the flag had been around long enough for every pirate ship in the country to steal or forge a copy, but she couldn't afford the fine for failing to adhere to regulations, and she certainly couldn't afford for the second ship to think they were pirates and fire on them.

She put down her cup, and ran up the staircase onto the main deck. Grabbing the flag from the storage cupboard under the wheel, she tucked it into her belt before beginning to climb the rigging. She was far from being, well, Tristan, but she made good progress up the network of ropes and eventually was on top of the sheet metal balloon that kept them afloat. She crouched and walked carefully along it, nervous that she would somehow pierce the thin metal and release the gas, which would be far more disastrous than not raising a flag, so she was glad when she'd swung up into the crow's nest. Tying the flag to the pole in the centre, she grabbed binoculars from her belt to check they had raised theirs also. In the time that it had taken her to climb, the other ship had gotten closer. The flag was flying high, but she wasn't entirely reassured. She looked around the deck, examining each of the crew in turn. They were all armed, which wasn't unusual – her whole crew owned guns and most carried them, including herself. Still there was an unsettling feeling in her gut, and her father had taught her that sometimes the brain subconsciously picks up clues that it can't consciously interpret... in other words, to trust her instincts.

She sighed. The crew was going to love her for this. Descending was easier than ascending, the gloves allowed her to slip down ropes without burning her hands. Running down into the corridor, she knocked the door to the crew room, Gloria's cabin, and Henry's cabin. To her amusement, Henry and Rob opened their doors at exactly the same time.

"Possible pirates approaching. Get dressed and armed, and on deck. Where the hell is Gloria?"

Henry coughed, and Mac peered past him into the room to see Gloria standing, wrapped in his sheet.

She stopped dead in shock, and was aware her mouth had dropped open a little.

"Morning, Captain," said Gloria sheepishly.

Rob started to laugh, which broke the tension. Mac just shook her head.

"Dressed, armed and on deck, people," she repeated. "I'll get Ethan."

The Spitfire Project

Rushing down another level, she went to knock on the workshop door, but Ethan opened it before she could, already dressed, though his hair was all over the place.

"Heard you running about upstairs," he required. "Do you want me to up the Arm a bit, see if we can get away?"

"Please."

The Arm was an invention of her fathers, which simply scooped coal from a store into the furnace, to keep the ship running without someone having to shovel it all the time. Ethan purposefully walked past her into the engine room.

Mac watched him go, quickly saying a prayer that she was wrong, before turning to run back up onto the deck, stopping quickly in her room to grab a pair of goggles from the desk, which she flung around her neck.

Full credit to her crew, they were all on deck already, looking alert.

"You've had a look?"

"Think you're probably right, Cap," said Gloria, determinedly trying not to look mortified.

"Well I guess there is one upside – I didn't interrupt you for nothing," grinned Mac, seeing the funny side now that she was over her shock. "Okay, business time. No one fire first, though I don't think that'll be a problem. Tristan, crow's nest, sharp shooting. And take down the stupid flag. Henry, at the wheel. Ethan's speeding us up so I want some quick maneuvering here – if we can get away without firing a shot, then I want to. James, cover Henry, make sure no one gets to him, so he can focus. Gloria, Rob... well, we've done this before, haven't we? Fight for your bloody lives. And goggles on, everyone."

There was a chorus of, "Yes, Captain," and before she had time to blink, Tristan was on the rigging and climbing with astounding speed.

Following her own advice, she pulled her goggles from her neck to over her eyes. If a bullet actually hit any of them, they'd be useless, but the last thing she wanted to do was to dodge bullets only to have an eye taken out by shrapnel.

The first bullet flew by her ear and hit the railing, which splintered. She took it as an invitation, aiming her gun at the rope that attached the pirate ship's balloon to the front of the deck. It hit home, and the rope unraveled a little, but didn't break.

She heard a shot from above and saw one of the pirates fall. *Nice work, Tristan.* The Spitfire began to accelerate, and Ethan appeared on deck.

"Sorry Captain, had some trouble with the Arm. Where do you want me?"

She grabbed a spare gun from her belt and threw it to him. "Just start shooting, Carlisle."

He dropped to his knees by the railing, aiming the pistol through the bars, and fired, not at the crew, but at the ship.

Any other captain might have questioned this, but Mac knew him well enough to know he had his own reasons, though she didn't understand them. Despite the Spitfire speeding up, the pirate ship gained on them. A grappling hook caught on the rigging and twisted into it. The Spitfire tilted a little as one of the pirates swung on it.

Carefully taking aim, Mac shot and watched as he let go and began to fall. But several more hooks soon followed. Tristan managed to shoot a few, as did she and James, but a pirates were at the side of the ship, scaling their ropes. They were out of Tristan's sightline, and when she peered over she was met with a hail of shots.

"*Shit.*"

She shot the first one to appear in the head, but then they were everywhere, and she knew the battle was no longer between two ships, but just on one.

CHAPTER SIX

Playing cards with the crew tonight was surprisingly fun. Even the captain, who most certainly hates me (the feeling is mutual) didn't attack me too much, she seems to have just decided to ignore my presence. Ethan Carlisle is lovely, I have no idea why he's on this ship. He should be at a university, or in business, you only need to look at his workshop to see he's brilliant.

The others are nice enough, but far more suited to this life. James Riddle flirts continuously, and I have no idea whether to take him seriously or not. Tristan Lynch is relaxed, easy to like.. It came up in conversation that his mother was black, which I should have guessed really. No one gets that tanned, even if they do work on an airship. I guess it's good that I've met Marcus Tate, as at least I know that there are intelligent, likeable Negroes. I hate to think how I would have embarrassed myself had Lynch been the first I'd really spoken to. Rob MacKinnon is friendly, with none of James' flirtation. Gloria and Henry I didn't speak to much. I think there is something going on between them – I wonder if Captain Sheridan knows that. I guess there are worse places to be, I certainly didn't expect people to be this kind when I realised I'd been kidnapped! All the same, I can't help wondering why I am here (Patrick Sheridan, who I have never heard of in my life, wanted to save me? It seems an unlikely story) and when I will be able to go home.

Sola didn't expect to sleep well, but the tension of the day had exhausted her to the point where she needed rest enough to forget her situation. But she woke with a start, unsure why. The mystery was soon solved, as there was another bang from above her, and then several more in succession.

Curious, and worried despite herself, she dressed quickly, not bothering with hair or make up, and ran up the stairs and out the door onto the deck.

Chaos. There were people everywhere, and she couldn't see the crew. There were bodies on the ground. Seeing one with long black hair, she ran towards it, pulling it over. She sighed with relief: it was a stranger, not Ethan. Then someone grabbed her shoulders and pulled her back. There was a shot behind her and whoever was holding her fell. She span around to see a strange man bleeding on the ground and Captain Sheridan staring grimly at her through red-lensed goggles.

"What the *hell* are you doing?! Get below!"

Her feet wouldn't move, and she just looked numbly back at the other woman, who pulled off her goggles and tossed them over. Somehow understanding, she pulled them onto her head, and was grateful a second later when the post beside her shattered and fragments of wood hit the lenses and her face, one embedding in her cheek.

This woke her out of her stupor, and she began to run. Mac ran towards her, barreling into her at full speed, knocking them both to the ground. She was shocked to feel blood on her face.

"Mine, not yours," said the captain roughly, and she saw a tear in the sleeve of Mac's shirt, which was being quickly stained with blood.

Sheridan pulled her up and ran with her, shoving her inside the door, which slammed behind her.

Sola began to hyperventilate and felt suddenly sick. She stumbled down the stairs, into her bedroom and then the en-suite, managing to make it to the toilet before vomiting. She curled up into a ball on the floor, trying and failing to control her breathing. The shots continued above her, and with every one she wondered if one of the crew was dead.

She didn't know how long passed before they stopped, but she still couldn't bring herself to move. Then there was a knock on her door. She didn't say anything, or try to get up, and she heard the creak of the hinges opening. Slow footsteps came closer and closer to her, until the person was standing in the doorway to the en suite.

"Sola," he said.

She finally was able to look, and let out the breath she'd been holding when she saw Ethan. He reached out a hand, and pulled her to her feet, then wrapped her in his arms.

"You're... is everyone?"

"A couple of injuries," he said bluntly, "but all alive. I was so scared when I saw you on the deck, why did you...?"

"I didn't... I thought... there was a body, I thought..."

He shushed her and cradled her to his chest, letting her sob into him. "Alright, everything's alright."

Eventually she calmed, and pulled back from the embrace.

"Come on. I've got to help treat the injuries down in the galley. I'll have a look at your cheek... and you should probably return those to the captain."

She looked down at her hand, having not even realised she was gripping the goggles tightly.

"She probably saved my eyesight," Sola admitted. "And then my life."

Ethan laughed. "Well, as she's pointed out several times, she didn't bring you aboard for her own entertainment."

"Yes but... I didn't believe her. I mean, a promise to her dying father? It just sounded so ridiculous."

"If she'd been lying, she would have made up something less ridiculous," Ethan reasoned.

"That's one way of looking at it, I guess," said Sola, still examining the goggles in her hands. "She's still a bitch."

Chuckling, Ethan just rolled his eyes. "Come on, let's get that splinter out."

Hand in hand they went down to the galley together. The kitchen had been transformed to a makeshift hospital. Captain Sheridan was sitting on a counter, with Gloria tending to her. The arm of her bloodstained shirt had been cut off to allow access to the wound. Sola wondered if she should make some enquiry after the captain's health, but in the first nice gesture she could remember, Mac saved her the awkwardness.

"It just grazed me," she said, grimacing as Gloria dabbed the injury with a sterilised rag.

She looked paler, smaller, and younger than Sola remembered, not like the bitch of the day before or the hard-faced captain she'd seen on deck during the fight.

"Your goggles," was all Sola said, reaching out her hand.

Smiling, Mac reached for them with her good arm. "Get Ethan to take that splinter out of your cheek. Don't want to ruin your good looks."

The final sentence was said with a little more of the sarcasm Sola had come to expect.

Ethan easily pulled out the fragment with a pair of tweezers.

"Shouldn't do any lasting damage," was his report. "Maybe a tiny scar. Do you have any other injuries?"

"Probably a few bruises from being shoved to the ground, but they'll sort themselves out."

He nodded, and rested his hand on top of hers. At first she pulled it away a little, out of instinct, but then she changed her mind and gripped it.

"I'm sorry you had to see that," he said. "Pirate attacks are pretty horrendous. They don't happen often."

"Scum of the earth," remarked James bitterly from behind him. "I fucking hate pirates."

Sola frowned in confusion. "So... you aren't pirates, then?"

The whole room burst into laughter, as Sola blushed.

Gloria was the first to contain herself, and said, "Give her a break. I suppose we did steal her from her room in the dead of night."

"This is a trade ship, Lady Austin," Mac said, hopping down from the counter. "You have a pretty romanticized idea of pirates if you think they'd be as kind to you as we've been. You'd be in the hold, not the captain's cabin. Riddle and Carlisle wouldn't be flirting with you, they'd have raped you. And you'd have a lot worse than a little splinter in your cheek. You may not like me much, but I assure you you're a lot better off than you would be if the pirates had taken this ship and their captain decided he was going to keep you around. You'd be praying for death."

With that statement, she nodded her thanks to Gloria, and left the room.

"She really brightens the mood, doesn't she?" said Gloria lightly.

There was some quiet laughter and slowly, conversation began again. No one seemed in a hurry to leave the galley. Rob was boiling water for tea over the stove, and Henry was still treating Tristan, who had a deep gash along his calf.

"This might keep you from swinging around for a while, mate," he said with a grimace.

Tristan forced a smile. "Not too long, I hope. I've got to earn my keep somehow."

"You earn your keep by working, like the rest of us," said Gloria sharply. "Mac's hardly going to dump you with the corpses."

"Corpses?" repeated Sola.

"I wouldn't recommend going up on deck right now," said Henry darkly.

The blood drained from her face. "Oh. How are you all alive? I mean, there were so many of them..."

"Disappointed?" asked James lightly.

"No!" Sola protested. "Just..."

"Don't joke, Riddle," Tristan interrupted. "You're no good at it. Lady Austin, those guys weren't exactly well trained. We keep in shape on the Spitfire, even Ethan can scale the rigging in half the time it would have taken most of those pirates. No one here smokes opium, we drink but we don't get drunk at work, ever – do you think they could all say the same? They're little better than scavengers, preying on small ships, assuming they'll be totally unprepared. But Patrick Sheridan was smarter than that, and so is his daughter, and so are we all."

Sola bowed her head in agreement.

"Well, I'm glad you are," she said.

She tried to stand but felt a searing pain in her ankle and fell back into her seat, letting out a string of expletives that her aunt would have murdered her for. Ethan was back at her side in an instant.

"Are you okay?"

"My ankle," she managed to gasp, as the pain slowly faded.

He tugged up the hem of her dress, and she looked down to see that the joint was purple and swollen.

"How the hell didn't I feel that?"

"Shock," said Gloria, who had turned and was kneeling down. "Bloody hell, these shoes are the most idiotic things I've ever seen, what were you thinking?"

Sola examined the black leather shoe, which wasn't particularly ornate, but did have a slight heel.

"I don't have any others here," she explained, though in honesty she hadn't even thought it through when she was dressing.

Gloria rolled her eyes at Ethan. "Seriously? You didn't pack her any shoes?"

"I was kind of distracted," he murmured. "Sorry, Sola."

"Hardly your fault," she said, wincing as Gloria prodded her ankle. "What do you reckon, will I live?"

Gloria chuckled.

"It's only a sprain. But get Mac to buy you some more sensible shoes when we're in Bristol," she critically eyed the girl in front of her. "And maybe clothes, for that matter."

Sola started to protest, but changed her mind, instead saying, "I don't have any money."

"She took you out of your home and away from your well stocked wardrobe," said Henry lightly. "I'm sure she won't object to buying you some shoes that won't kill you."

"I wouldn't be so certain," mumbled Sola darkly.

"I'll tell her," said Gloria, taking pity. "James, pass me a bandage so I can strap up Lady Austin's ankle."

CHAPTER SEVEN

Stopped by a small town and found an undertaker who agreed to take care of the bodies for a very reasonable price. Was worried about Lady Austin being noticed, but she stayed below the whole time – James told me that she was aware there were corpses on the deck, so that makes sense I guess. We've also cleaned up all the blood, so the Spitfire is back to her shining self. It's been so long since we had a pirate attack. Only about a month if you count when Father was killed, but he seemed to think that wasn't just pirates.

I still remember my first so clearly... unless there were some when I was too young to know what was happening. At fifteen years old, you would think that killing a man would haunt you, but it was not *killing him that haunted me. Father may have only been injured, but if he had been killed then, for my hesitation, I never could have forgiven myself. I suppose there was no way for me to win that day.*

And now I am organising my thoughts again (this log is useful, who would have imagined), I remember this morning's revelation – by which I mean, Gloria Wright and Henry Large are together! I should have seen that coming. As the two 'older' ones left aboard, along with the fact they have always been close, it was sort of inevitable. So long as the relationship stays good, it shouldn't be a problem. If it doesn't... well, I have enough real issues right now, I don't have time for hypothetical ones.

With a quiet sigh, Mac considered going along to the lounge and socialising with the crew, but just the thought drained her of any energy. Wandering over to her drawers, she pulled out a tumbler and a bottle of whiskey, remembering how her father had kept them in the same place, remembering how he had once said, "Sometimes you need to drink alone," and she had thought it sounded very sad.

The reality was even sadder.

She poured a double shot and put the bottle away, taking her drink out onto the back balcony, where her mug from the morning was still lying, and spilt coffee was all over the wood. Leaning over the railing, she sipped at the whiskey and stared at the stars, marvelling at how her day could begin and end in the same place as though nothing had happened in it at all. Her arm throbbed with pain, gently reminding her of what had.

The next two days contained no major incidents, for which Mac couldn't have been more grateful. Austin spent most of her time in Ethan's workshop, which suited everyone just fine. Tristan began to recover a little and instantly wanted to push himself past his limits, everyone pitched in to stop him. Henry and Gloria continued as usual, giving no hint that their relationship had been discovered. Mac had no idea if this was because it was easiest for them, or if it was because they thought it would be easiest for everyone else, but, again, it worked. And one morning, the city of Bristol appeared on the horizon.

"Austin, I'm going to have to tighten your security when we're in the city," Mac said, putting down a card on the table. "You'll have someone with you at all times, and I'm going to lock your door at night."

"You really think that's necessary?" said Ethan, putting down his next card and trumping her instantly.

"Yes, Mr Carlisle, I really do."

Her tone left absolutely no room for discussion.

Sola said nothing, carefully considering her hand. It was the first game she'd played without Ethan helping out.

"No snide remarks?" Mac asked. "No angry rants? Not going to try to slap me?"

"If I thought you were anything less than unyielding, Captain Sheridan, I would try," she replied coldly.

"Why, Lady Austin, was that a compliment?"

Placing down a card, Sola said in a measured tone, "I certainly didn't intend it as one."

Mac smirked.

"I fold," she said, placing down her hand. "Sleep well, everyone, we'll be in Bristol tomorrow."

She didn't relax until she got back to the study and collapsed into the chair at her desk, sinking her head into her hands. The exhaustion was getting impossible to manage. She hadn't stayed through a whole card game for the past few days. Luckily, her crew was assuming it was to get away from Austin, who they seemed to like even more after the pirate attack. Mac still found her irritating, but she was glad for the misdirection, otherwise she expected that Gloria, at least, would have realised something was wrong.

Gloria had given her a firm directive to buy Austin some more practical clothes and shoes. As much as she resented the idea, Mac saw the sense in it. She would have to try and fit it in between loading, unloading, and meeting with businesses... just at the thought, she dropped her head onto the desk and groaned.

Bristol was one of her favourite cities. The airship docks were directly about the marine docks, and being by the sea had always suited her. The dockers were always up early, and free for a chat in the mornings.

"Mornin' love," one greeted as she descended onto the lower dock.

The pet names had once driven her crazy, but she had come to see there was no harm in them.

"Morning, mate," she responded.

"You work up on them airships?"

"Just on the one," Mac smiled. "The Spitfire's my baby."

His eyebrows rose into his hairline. "You captain?"

"I am that."

He took a few seconds to digest this information. It was more accepted for women to work on airships than at sea, and the number of female captains was steadily increasing, so she doubted she was the first he'd met, but she was probably one of the first.

"Where you flying from then, Captain?"

She perched on a crate. "London this time."

"Did you hear about the lady disappeared?" came another voice from behind her, voice full of excitement.

Her heart thumped. "Nah, don't get any news in transit. What happened?"

"Vanished, din't she?" said another worker, joining it. "Just wasn't there one night. Aunt's claiming she must've been kidnapped, but a load of 'er clothes are gone too."

"Prob'ly run off with someone," said the first man. "Hey, maybe she had a Moor lover, huh?"

He elbowed the black man beside him with that comment, and laughed loudly at himself.

"Are you lot reading romance novels by candlelight?" Mac laughed.

"Whole thing don't make any sense," commented the second man. "But I don't give a damn. Fucking lords and ladies everywhere all the time – I'd like to see them work here for a day."

Mac burst out laughing. "That would be a sight, for damn sure."

"Maybe it'll happen if them anarchists have their way," he grinned.

Her laughter died. "Didn't realise news of that lot had spread this far."

"You joking? After the bombs the other month, s'all people have been talking about."

She nodded, quietly feeling sick at the thought. Fifty people had been killed at a ball – a few of them aristocrats, but mostly servants or slaves who had been working.

"I've been across trading on the Continent, I have a lot to catch up on," she said by way of explanation.

"International trade," said one of the men, sounding impressed. "Careful you don't put yourself in competition with Bingley's."

"I wouldn't go near Edward Bingley's area of expertise for all the money in the world."

He nodded. "Wise enough, Captain. Couple of my mates have burnt all their wages on the foul stuff. They don't have jobs any more neither, but they still want it all the time. S'evil."

"That it is," she said. "Good chatting, gentlemen, but I've got some meetings in the city to prepare for, and I should make sure my crew get there arses out of bed some time soon."

There was a round of laughter, and she ascended the steps again, with some food for thought. Sola Austin going out at all was obviously going to be a problem. And as for the anarchism... Marcus wondered why she didn't like them! But their ideas were spreading like wildfire, there was no denying that. Never mind Edward Bingley's opium smuggling. That was old enough news, but no one was ever going to challenge Britain's king of trade on the shady side of his business.

Tristan was awake, clambering around the rigging as part of his personal mission to be back to full fitness as soon as possible.

"Lynch! You want food?"

He was down within a few seconds. "Sounds great, Captain. You not eaten?"

"Not yet. Let's get breakfast then wake the rest of them and let Austin out of her room."

"You really think she's going to try and escape?" he asked, sounding interested but not argumentative, to her relief.

Mac sighed and indicated they should begin to walk down the galley.

"I know you guys get on with her, and I'm glad, I am," she paused, aware she hadn't sounded convincing in the slightest. "But at the end of the day, she's here against her will. I'm not going to take the chance that your company is charming enough to make her want to stay."

"Not even Carlisle's company?" he said with a grin.

She laughed.

"You called that one right, for sure. Has James given you your money?"

"He says they aren't actually together yet," Tristan shrugged. "I'll wait. You taking Austin out to get clothes today?"

She opened the galley and began to rummage around in the cupboards, with Tristan following suit.

"If I have a spare hour or two. I'm going to have to disguise her somehow, the news of her disappearance is everywhere."

"Should have guessed it'd be that way, I s'pose."

"I don't have to like it, though. How's her ankle?"

"Improving. She's still borrowing Gloria's shoes, Gloria won't let her wear the heels."

Mac laughed, marvelling at how much she was managing to miss out on.

"Do they fit?"

"They're a bit big, I think."

"They'll do till we get her her own. C'mon, you want to wake people up?"

His smile had an evil edge to it.

"Be my pleasure, Captain."

She tossed him the key to Sola's room. "Get the lady too. But make sure she stays below deck. Shove her into the workshop once Ethan's made himself decent," she paused for a second. "Or before, if you want your money any time soon."

CHAPTER EIGHT

We're arriving in Bristol tomorrow morning, which means Captain Sheridan is going to start locking me in this room at night, and ensuring I am never left alone. I'm already looking forward to it. Thankfully she seems to avoid me as much as possible, not even spending any real time in the crew lounge. I know I should feel guilty at displacing her, but instead I feel a sort of, well, glee, I think would be the best way to put it. The woman did kidnap me, so I'm not averse to causing her a little discomfort.

My ankle still hurts to walk on, but the swelling and bruising have gone down. I'll be glad if I can get some boots of my own while we're in the city, because wearing Gloria's is giving me blisters.

The crew (barring the captain) truly seems to have accepted me now, which is both very nice and very strange. I guess Captain Sheridan was right about my view of piracy – having had a very brief up-close glimpse of them now, any impressions of 'loveable rogues' I may have had are well and truly dissipated. That makes it all the more pleasant to be with a group of what seem to be genuinely good people.

I just heard a key turn in my lock – I guess I really am a prisoner for now! The thought makes me boil with rage, though there is a part of me that understands... I suppose, if for some ridiculous reason, I ended up kidnapping someone, I'd do everything in my power to prevent them from escaping also.

There was a sharp and constant tapping on the door, waking Sola from her doze.

"What?" she said sharply, as she'd been enjoying the half-dream state.

In her dreams she'd been back in the guesthouse with Jesse, just talking and laughing as they'd done on occasion. She felt a pang in her chest, missing his company. She'd been so nervous about seeing him after the night they spent together, but now she'd like nothing more, no matter how awkward it might be.

"Door's unlocked, just letting you know," came Tristan's cheerful voice from behind the door. "Good morning to you too!"

She groaned and rolled over, but knew instantly that she wouldn't be able to sleep again. Cursing, she got herself out of bed and pulled on a dressing gown that Ethan had lent her. She felt like a bath before she made the effort of getting ready, even though she'd likely spent the whole day inside the Spitfire because of Captain Sheridan's paranoia.

She heated water on the stove in the crew bathroom and carried it through, a method that she had quickly adapted to, shocking even herself, and once it was the right temperature, locked the en suite door and sank into the hot water.

Sola would have liked the chance to explore Bristol, where she'd never been, but she didn't expect to get it. The most she could hope for was that Sheridan would be busy enough with her captain-business in the city to be totally out of the way for a little while.

After dressing and eating breakfast, Sola automatically headed for the workshop. At least in there, she could talk to Ethan, and the rest of the crew would stop eyeing her suspiciously, as though she were going to run at any second. She'd come to get on so well with them, and hated the reminder that they were captors as well as friends.

"Morning, Ethan," she said, sitting at a chair next to the table where he was working.

He looked as though he'd dressed in a hurry, with his top button undone and his black hair in a tangled mess. By now, she recognised the symptoms of being engrossed in an invention, and wasn't offended when she only got a grunt in reply.

She sipped at the coffee she'd brought through and examined the desk, which was unfailingly filled with interesting things, though she didn't understand most of them. After about forty-five minutes, he clicked two components together and his face split into a wide smile.

"Good morning, Sola," he said brightly. "That one kept me up most of the night. How did you sleep?"

The Spitfire Project

"Well," she said, suddenly blushing and feeling an odd wave of guilt when she thought of her dream. "Here let me sort..." she reached out and ran her fingers through his hair, mumbling to herself. "I need a hairbrush, I can barely fix my own but I should really be able to..." her finger snagged on a not, and he gasped sharply. "Sorry, it's just in such a state..."

Eventually her hands slowed and she fell silent as she realised what she was doing. She snatched her arms back at great speed.

"God, I'm so sorry, I don't know what I was thinking."

He smiled at her. "It's fine. It does get in a bit of a mess."

There was a tension in the air that neither of them knew how to address.

"Erm, I..." Ethan began.

"Yeah, definitely," agreed Sola quickly. "I'd quite like another coffee, do you want a cup of tea?"

"That'd be great," Ethan said. "I'll come with you."

"No, that's fine."

"Really, I should..."

She raised her eyebrows. "Ethan. I swear I'm not going to make a break for freedom. I'm going to make a cup of coffee for me, and tea for you, and be back in a few minutes. Trust me."

He swallowed, but nodded.

Sola was glad to escape the room. She'd never dealt well with that sort of situation. There was no doubt she liked Ethan, he'd been very kind to her from day one, and was her closest friend aboard the Spitfire. His mind was incredible, you only had to watch him work to see he was a rare breed of genius. The feeling of his hair under her fingers came back to her, and she felt the blood rush to her face again. Oh this was bad. This was really bad.

She tried to shake some sense into herself, and focused on the immediate task of tea and coffee. The lower level of the ship was empty, so luckily no one was around to question why she was so red in the face – she knew immediately what James, at least, would think.

By the time the drinks were made, she at least felt she'd returned to almost her normal colour, and composed herself enough to go back in the room without stammering more horrific apologies. She didn't even know what she was apologising for, except that she'd crossed a line that friends shouldn't, and now wanted the impossible – to go back to how it had been before.

She had to try, if she didn't want to lose Ethan completely. She slipped quietly into the workshop, only to find it empty.

"Ethan?"

"Round the corner," came his voice, and she felt a rush of relief.

He was sitting at the desk on the other side of the room, writing. It was an unusual sight.

"What's that?" she asked, sitting the cup of tea beside him and perching up on the nearest worktable.

"I'm filling out a patent," he said, putting down the pen and sighing. "How is it that no matter what you end up doing, you can never escape paperwork?"

Sola laughed. "I wouldn't know."

"I suppose you wouldn't."

He frowned.

"What?"

"I was just wondering... what was on the cards for you before we so rudely interrupted your life? I somehow can't imagine you marrying some nice aristocrat and having a couple kids. Paying visits. Entertaining guests. Embroidering... but then, I've never seen you in that environment."

As he spoke, the smile had faded from Sola's face. It was a problem that had been on her mind ever since she turned eighteen. The life Ethan had described may have been where she ended up if it weren't for Jesse, but after year of spying, and of being oddly more relaxed with a group of anarchists in a guest house than at balls or dinner parties, the thought of it repelled her. She had avoided or put off any of the men her aunt had tried to introduce her... but all the same she would have had to make a decision at some point. A few times, she was tempted to just pack a bag and go live with Jesse. Maybe she would have, if she'd known he'd have her.

"I can't imagine that either," she said truthfully. "But there weren't many options."

She felt guilty, even though she wasn't technically lying to him.

The Spitfire Project

Though she did trust Ethan, she didn't want him to know about Jesse, nor did she want to put him in a situation where he had to decide between Captain Sheridan and herself.

"I'm glad..." he trailed off.

"That there weren't many options?" she asked, confused.

He shook his head, laughing a little, and his cheeks coloured.

"That you aren't married," he clarified, breaking eye contact.

Sola was shocked into silence, and he muttered something, turning back to his paperwork.

"Well, if I were, you'd have an angry husband to be dealing with right now," she said, trying to break the awkwardness.

Ethan snorted.

"That's not what I meant."

She rested her hand on his forearm.

"I know," leaning forward, she pressed her lips to his cheek, and then moved them to his ear. "I'm glad too," she whispered. Surprised by her own boldness, she squeezed his arm and said, "I'm just going to fetch my journal – it's as close to paperwork as I get."

Sola needn't have feared that the rest of the day would be tense. Nothing more happened, but they sat together in the workshop, occasionally conversing, otherwise working in silence. She was comfortable with both, which was strange considering how on edge she'd always been around Jesse. Then again, Ethan didn't have the same dangerous vibe, like his mood could change at any minute.

At one point there was a loud noise from below them, and Sola was briefly confused until Ethan explained that it was the hold opening to be unloaded.

"Sounds like I need to oil the hinges," he mused aloud.

She giggled at the thought, and said, "You just usually work so delicately, it's hard to imagine," by way of explanation.

"I don't let the others near any mechanism if I can avoid it," he grinned. "I don't trust them."

In the early evening, there was a tap at the door.

"Come on in," said Ethan.

Captain Sheridan walked into the room, carrying a large grey cloak over her arm.

"How's your ankle, Lady Austin?"

"Significantly improved," Sola replied, back straightening as it always did around the captain.

"Up for a walk into the city?"

"Why?"

"Gloria demanded you be given more appropriate clothing," she said, rolling her eyes.

Sola nodded. The thought of spending any length of time with Captain Sheridan wasn't appealing, but the idea of shoes that fit her was.

"Now?"

"Yes, put this on," Mac said, throwing the cloak over at Sola. "Wear the hood up, and look at the ground, and don't dare let anyone see your face."

Sola sighed in exasperation, and threw it around her shoulders. It was a good quality garment, with a fur-trimmed hood that she pulled up over her head.

"Does that work for you, Captain Sheridan?"

"It'll have to. Ethan, feel free to take the next few hours off and actually get some fresh air for once."

Sola wanted Ethan to be offended, but he just laughed.

"Yes, Captain."

It didn't take long before Sola could see why the cloak was necessary. Her face was on every newspaper they passed. Captain Sheridan explained in a low tone all the rumours that were going around, her voice tinted with amusement as she described the theory that she'd ran off with a black lover.

Sola almost laughed with her, but then she remembered herself, and clamped her mouth shut. The captain led her with confidence through the city, eventually into back streets lined with less affluent shops. There were beggars sitting in the gutters, groaning pathetically.

"Won't you give them some change?" she asked, feeling a surge of pity.

"No."

The complete lack of hesitation startled her.

"Are you so completely heartless?"

Mac stopped in the middle of the street and fixed her with a harsh glare. She turned to one of the beggars, a thin, wasted man.

"You, sir, were you a docker or a factory worker?"

The figure whimpered.

"Answer me, man."

Sola watched, horrified but unable to look away.

"A docker," the man eventually croaked.

"You have a family, I assume?"

He nodded.

"Wife? Children?"

"Yes. Please ma'am..."

"Are they in the workhouses now?"

He buried his head in his hands. Mac shook hers, catching Sola's eye. She pulled a few coins from a pocket in her utility belt, and crouched down, pressing them into the hand of the pathetic figure. He scrambled to his feet and stumbled away as fast as he could.

"He's going to buy opium," Mac said softly. "So tell me, Lady Austin, was it kind, what I just did? The man is going to die soon, he'll never see his family again. There is an argument for it being kind, to allow him to forget for a while. But that money will go to an opium den, who will use it to import the drug, allowing them to hook more men who want to escape some of the misery of their lives, causing more children in workhouses. Most of those children will die. Some might make it to being factory workers or dockers, working day and night to just scrape enough money to feed and house their families, and maybe one day they will be drawn to the same drug that killed their fathers, just to escape for a few hours the misery of their lives. So was it kind?"

Sola just stared at her, incapable of speech.

"Come on, Lady Austin," Mac said, beginning to walk. "I expect we shall be robbed by some other desperate soul if we linger here any longer."

A way up the next street, Mac stopped and knocked the door of a shop that looked as though it had been shut down years before.

"We're closed! Go away!" a woman yelled from inside.

"Open the bloody door, Tam!" Mac yelled in return.

After a couple of seconds, it was flung open, to reveal a slightly mad looking middle aged woman, and a room full of clothes.

"Mackenzie Sheridan," she said, her face spreading into a grin. "Bloody hell."

The two women reached out and embraced each other.

"You could have warned me you were visiting," said 'Tam' when they parted.

"Oh, where's the fun in that?" joked Mac.

The older woman snorted.

"Typical. Come in come in come in. Who's your friend?"

"I can't say friend is the word I'd use," mumbled Mac, glancing over at Sola.

"No, nor me," said Sola, stepping inside and closing the door behind her.

Lights flickered on around the shop.

"Let me see you, Mac," said Tam, "step into the light. I haven't seen you for a good year."

"Two," Mac corrected.

"And you still haven't outgrown those clothes?"

She laughed.

"Please, I haven't grown since I was about fourteen. I could do with a new jacket though. A smarter one. For..." she trailed off.

"I heard," said the woman softly. "I'm so sorry for your loss. I loved your father like a brother, you know that."

"I do," said Mac. "And I know he loved you as a sister."

"You'll do a grand job of captaining that lovely ship, I know you will."

"Thanks," Mac replied, closing the conversation. She looked back at Sola. "You can take the hood down."

Although she bristled, Sola followed the instruction. The shopkeeper looked over to her and frowned, then gasped.

"Oh please tell me that's not..."

Mac pinched the bridge of her nose.

"I wish I could. Lady Austin, this is my good friend and tailor,

Tamsin Worthing. Tam... Lady Sola Austin."

"What on earth have you done?"

"Do you trust me, Tamsin?" asked Mac seriously.

"I..." she faltered, and then regained herself. "Of course I do."

They shared a look of mutual understanding.

"Lady Austin needs some practical clothing for airship wear. Also shoes. Can you help us?"

As she got over her shock, Tamsin smirked.

"Do you really have to ask?"

For the next hour, Tamsin fussed over Sola, measuring her and flitting around the shop and storeroom, which were bursting at the seams with different fabrics and garments. At the end of it she had been given a pair of long leather boots, a pair of short leather boots, two pairs of breeches, four comfortable shirts, and a solid jacket.

She changed in the storeroom into these more practical clothes, and examined herself in a dusty mirror. Clothing shouldn't change how she looked, but it did. She also noticed that her skin was slightly darker than it had been the week before.

She walked back out into the shop to see Mac paying Tamsin.

"I'll visit again soon," the younger woman promised. "When this whole mess is sorted out, we'll have a drink together."

"You better," Tamsin warned. "But hold your horses for two seconds, I have something for you."

She disappeared into the storeroom again. Sola gave Mac a questioning look, to which she shrugged her shoulders. With a start, Sola realised it was the first non-confrontational interaction they'd had.

When Tamsin reappeared, there was a jacket over her arm.

"Try it on?"

Mac complied, shrugging off her leather flying jacket and pulling it on. It was red, double breasted, and reached to mid-way down her thighs. The buttons were brass and it was trimmed in gold thread. Grudgingly, Sola thought to herself that it looked very official, and suited the captain completely.

"I... how much?" Mac asked.

"It's paid for," said Tamsin.

"I can't let you do that, Tam," she protested.

"Not by me, Mac," smiled the woman. "Your father wrote to me, commissioning me to make it. He paid for it. You see..." she paused, as if wondering whether to continue, but then went for it, "he was going to make you captain. Not right away, perhaps. But within the next few years. He believed you could do it."

Sola watched in wonder as a whole range of inexplicable emotions passed over Mackenzie Sheridan's face.

"Thank you," she whispered.

CHAPTER NINE

I was thrown by the idea that Father planned to hand over the captaincy to me. Did he really think I was capable of this? I'm barely managing. Though I suppose he thought he would be around to advise me. I wish he were, and not just because I miss him. I could certainly do with an advisor. Anyway, there is no point in dwelling on my inadequacies. This is my job, and I have to do it, and that's all there is to it.

No matter how many times I see it, the sight of opium-riddled beggars repels me. I hope it haunts Lady Austin also – the aristocracy must take no small part of the blame for this disease of society.

Mac felt a familiar surge of anger as she considered the situation, but she forced it back down. She couldn't work herself into a state over opium the week before a trade conference where she'd have to look Edward Bingley in the eye.

Thinking of the conference made her look over at the jacket Tamsin had given her, which was lying out on top of drawers. It was a good quality garment, well made (as was anything from Tamsin Worthing), and very smart. She couldn't help slipping it on again, looking down at herself. Smiling, she straightened her shoulders.

This was her job. And she'd just have to do it.

Shedding the jacket again, she left the study to join her crew for a drink in the lounge. Oddly, in her new clothes, with a glass of wine and a hand of playing cards, Sola Austin almost looked like one of the crew herself.

"Hey, Cap," greeted James, "where's Rob gotten himself off to?"

"I gave him tonight off," she said as she poured a cider.

"So he does have a lover in the city then?" he asked.

She raised her eyebrows.

"I don't know and I don't want to know, Riddle. Do you need him for something?"

"Just moral support," Gloria said with a grin. "Sola's trouncing him."

Mac laughed in surprise.

"This I have to see."

"Are you sure you don't want us to start a new game, Cap?" James pleaded. "So you can play?"

"Have I ever been that nice to you?"

"You're going to let me lose all my money?"

"Some day you should accept that you're really bad at gambling," Mac said. "This is tough love. Also Lady Austin might be glad to have some of her own money to spend when we hit Glasgow."

Sola whirled around in surprise.

"You're going to let me out?"

"Only if someone's with you. But in your new attire we can probably pass you off as crew, though you might not want to speak too much. Your voice gives you away."

"That's a change of heart," said Sola, still sounding as though she didn't entirely trust what she was hearing.

"Well, I think Ethan might want to take you out," Mac smirked. "It'd be cruel of me to deny him the opportunity."

James laughed, while Ethan groaned.

"Brilliant, Cap," remarked the former.

"Thank you, James," she replied. "I'd bow out gracefully soon, by the way."

"Never," he grinned.

She just shook her head.

"Go on then, Lady Austin," she remarked. "Make it quick, this is painful."

With an evil smile, Austin laid out the rest of her cards, to laughter and applause from the room. James sank his head into his hands.

"Cough up, Riddle," said Henry, thumping the younger man on the back. "Lose with grace."

The Spitfire Project

Mac saw Gloria was giving him an odd look, and frowned at the other woman. When Gloria noticed Mac was looking at her, she just shook her head. Knowing better than to press the issue, Mac shrugged in reply.

She turned instead to study Sola Austin, something that was becoming a frequent and unwelcome past time. The girl tucked a lock of hair behind her ear, and then her hand drifted down to a chain around her neck. Mac had never noticed the necklace before. It was a locket with an engraving of a dragonfly on it.

"Nice necklace," said Gloria, having also noticed the motion.

"Thanks," said Sola, with a sad smile. "It was my mothers."

"What happened to her?"

Mac kept quiet, listening with interest but feeling that if she joined in, she would kill the conversation immediately.

"She died," Sola said. She waited a few seconds in indecision. Then she continued. "She killed herself, actually." Her voice was mixture of bitterness and sorrow. "In an asylum."

The room fell completely silent. Sola was looking at her lap, and then she raised her head and glared defiantly out at them.

"Go on," she challenged. "Say what you're thinking."

"We're not thinking anything, Sola," said Ethan gently, "except that we're terribly sorry."

They all nodded their agreement, still not trusting themselves to speak.

"I was just a baby," Sola said, the anger gone. "I didn't know her or anything."

"She was still your mother," said Gloria. "Do you have a photo of her in there?"

Sola nodded, unclipping the chain behind her neck.

"And of my father – he died before I was born."

She clicked open the locket and handed it to Gloria.

"What a good-looking couple," said the older woman. "They look very in love."

"Everyone tells me they were," smiled Sola.

"May I?" asked Mac, stretching out her hand.

Sola gave her a look of extreme suspicion, before nodding her assent. The instant she saw the photo, recognition flooded Mac, and excitement coursed through her, and she did her best not to show either, in case she was wrong. She handed the necklace back.

"Sorry for your loss," she said, hoping the other girl wouldn't think she was being sarcastic (though she couldn't blame her if she did think so). "Excuse me."

It was all she could do not to run back to the study. On a shelf were all her father's books, and she selected one that she had frequently seen him with, although not reading. Opening it to the back cover, she pulled out an old photograph. She wasn't sure if she'd forgotten about it completely, or just had no reason to think of it until now. On one side was her father, looking younger than she'd ever known him, his beard barely stubble, and next to him a woman she knew was her mother, although they'd never met. On the other side were another man and woman that she now knew to be Sola Austin's parents. The four were standing on the deck of the Spitfire, smiling widely at the camera. Mac flipped over the photo and read the handwriting on the back - "Us with Bea and George when we took them to their country house" - the writing wasn't her father's, which she would have guessed even if she didn't have plenty to compare it to. He, at least, would have been methodical enough to write the date of the photograph.

Holding the photo, she stepped out into the corridors, somehow knowing that she should show the photo to Lady Austin. With a start, she realised that Sola might recognise her father. There was a chance they had met at some point. She had never known her father to meet aristocrats – but there was obviously a lot she didn't know about him. The idea pained her, but it was true. She'd never heard of "Bea and George", who her parents were apparently friends with. She'd never heard him mention Sola Austin, yet he'd made her promise to save the woman's life. And he'd never mentioned making her captain before his death, but apparently he'd been planning for it. What was there to say he hadn't snuck away sometime they were in London and met with Austin? She had to check. She stuck her head around the door.

"Lady Austin, a word?"

She could see the other woman roll her eyes, and bit back a sarcastic comment of her own. Once Austin was out in the corridor and the door was closed, she handed over the photo.

"When I looked at your photo, I knew I recognised your parents from somewhere. That's them with..." she swallowed, "with my parents."

There was disbelief in Austin's eyes, and Mac couldn't blame her. But the evidence was there, black and white.

"I have to ask, did you ever meet my father before he died?"

"No."

"Are you sure? He'd have been older, obviously. He had a beard, and grey in his hair."

"Never, I'm certain. I don't understand..."

"No, nor do I. Though it might explain why Father wanted me to save your life."

"I suppose. I... thank you for sharing this with me, Captain Sheridan."

"Well, I couldn't help hoping you'd be more useful than you were," Mac said with her usual sarcasm, though none of the edge that was normally present.

Sola snorted.

"You're not exactly a fount of knowledge yourself." She looked back at the photo, and smiled. "I don't have many photographs of my parents," she explained. "They look pretty happy here."

"Keep it," Mac replied, surprising herself.

"Seriously?"

"I have plenty of Father. And I never knew Mother, so it doesn't matter so much, but I have a few."

"What happened to her?"

Mac eyed Sola critically before deciding that she'd discovered plenty about the other girl's family that evening.

"She died in childbirth," she said shortly.

"I'm sorry."

"Me too. But I had Father. You were raised by your aunt, right?"

"Yes, my Aunt Judith. We don't get on, really."

"No, I wouldn't imagine so."

Sola gave her a curious frown.

"What makes you say that?"

Mac nodded toward the door to the crew lounge.

"You get on far too well with that lot to have fitted in much in London."

Sola smiled.

"Very perceptive, Captain Sheridan."

"Go back to your game, Lady Austin," said Mac. "Make Riddle cry. And let me know if you have any revelations."

"Will do, Captain."

Mac felt something had been strange about the conversation, and then realised that Austin had called her "Captain", rather than her usual formal "Captain Sheridan".

For some odd reason, that made her smile.

CHAPTER TEN

I can't stop looking at the photograph of my parents with Captain Sheridan's parents. I wish that I were at home, so I could search through my photo album for any sign of them. I wonder if they were at my parents' wedding.. I wish I had more photos of Mother and Father. I think Aunt Judith may have destroyed many of them in her grief, although she would never confirm if she had. Though I didn't know them, I still keenly feel the loss.

It was kind of Captain Sheridan to give me the photos. And 'kind' is not a word I have ever associated with Captain Sheridan before. Who knows, maybe she felt guilty for the lecture she gave me about beggars earlier – though somehow I doubt that.

I love my new clothes. I mean, there are a few of my dresses I never want to part with, but the comfort and practicality of breeches and shirts and boots is incredible. Additionally, I feel even more as though I fit in aboard the Spitfire. I trounced James at cards tonight and have the money in my pocket to prove it (another triumph of practicality – pockets!) and Captain Sheridan will apparently actually let me out with Ethan in Glasgow.

Speaking of Ethan, I have accepted the idea of there being something between us. It may come to nothing, but I've decided to let things run their course one way of the other, and stop worrying about Jesse. I do miss him, but in reality I have no idea when I will see him next, and it is a little nice to be away from the confusion of trying to work out where I stand with him.

Sola was relieved to have left Bristol. There was a freedom to being, as Captain Sheridan put it, 'in transit'. Gloria disagreed, saying they were stuck on board the ship, and that wasn't freedom. It was an understandable point, but all the same, Sola disagreed.

She still spent most of her time in the workshop with Ethan. When he was absorbed, she would contemplate the mystery of her parents. Her father had died in a factory fire several months before she was born. Her mother was diagnosed with "insanity due to childbirth" before she was even six months old, and was incarcerated in Bethlem Hospital – or 'Bedlam'. Within a few weeks, she was found dead in her room. No one had ever told Sola the details, and she wasn't sure whether she wanted to know or not. Somehow before their deaths they'd known Patrick Sheridan and his wife... she related all this to Ethan, in case he could see a connection she didn't.

"They never married," was all Ethan said.

"Sorry?"

"Patrick and Aislin weren't married," he reiterated.

"Aislin?" she said sharply.

"Mac's mother."

"You are joking."

"No?"

She shook her head in disbelief.

"That's my middle name," she explained.

"Wow. They must have been pretty good friends then," said Ethan.

"They must have been. So why have I never heard of them? And Captain Sheridan's never heard of my parents either.'"

"You're going in circles here, Sola," he pointed out gently.

"I just can't get my head around it."

He sighed and put down his pen, turning to give her his full attention.

"Think," he said. "Not about your parents, about you. Something changed. You were safe, and then you weren't. What happened?"

And Sola knew this was the moment that she had to decide. She either trusted him or she didn't. She bit her lip.

"I met some people," she said. "Anarchists."

"Dear god, Sola," he replied, closing his eyes. "You didn't think that was worth mentioning before?"

"Look, kidnapping people isn't exactly a great way to earn their trust, okay," she snapped.

He nodded.

"Go on."

"I started helping them out. Just... picking up gossip, looking through people's papers for evidence of corruption or some information that could be used against them..."

"What on *earth* made you think that was a good idea?"

"Look, there's merit in the arguments. When you hear the stories of what some of these people have been through, you can't *help* thinking that if that's what our government does, we're better off without one!"

"And did you think for one second about the danger you were putting yourself in? They're *outlaws*, Sola, they're ruthless criminals!"

"They are *not* ruthless."

"And I suppose the bombings last month were a bit of harmless fun?"

"That wasn't them."

"Oh wake up. Who was it then?"

"It wasn't them."

Sola clung to that. She'd been at the country house when she heard about the bombings, and had immediately written to one of the anarchists she was close with, a woman named Charity. Charity had written back, assuring her they had had no part in it, but couldn't come forward to protest their innocence, as they'd simply be arrested for being anarchists.

"Do you have proof of that?"

"I don't need proof, I know them."

"Of course you do."

"Get over yourself, Ethan. You don't get to be angry that I maybe wasn't completely the stereotypical aristocratic brat you all assumed I would be."

"I never for a second thought you were, in fact, I assumed you had more brains than this!"

She stood.

"Fuck this, I'm not going to fight with you."

"Tell the captain," he ordered

"Why should I?" she shot back childishly.

"Tell her, or I will."

Spinning on her heel, Sola stormed out of the workshop.

She seethed in her room for a good two hours, but she knew that eventually she did have to tell Captain Sheridan, and not because Ethan said so, but because she was beginning to realise that they would only get answers if they shared information with each other. They both had part of the story, and it was time to start putting it together. She stepped out of her room and looked at the door opposite, which she knew was the captain's study, one of the few rooms left on the Spitfire that she hadn't set foot in.

From Ethan's reaction, she guessed the captain wouldn't be thrilled, but she steeled herself and knocked.

"Come in," came the muffled voice.

Curiosity mounting, she twisted the handle and stepped inside. The study was half the size of her own room. In one corner was a large desk with a porthole in front of it, and papers spread across it. There was a mezzanine to the side, with a mattress on it and a blanket hanging off the edge. Beneath the mezzanine was a chest of drawers, and to one side was a circular table with two chairs. In the corner was another door, and she wondered briefly where it led to.

Captain Sheridan was sitting at the desk, and she turned around.

"Lady Austin. I suppose I'll take even your company over keeping the books."

"Your manners continue to be sublime, Captain Sheridan."

Mac laughed.

"Can I offer you a coffee? I made a pot earlier when it became all too clear this afternoon was going to descend into paperwork."

"Please," said Sola, feeling a sudden caffeine craving now that it had been mentioned.

Mac walked under the mezzanine, pulling a mug from the top drawer. She poured coffee into it and placed it on the circular table, then grabbed her own mug from the desk and topped it up.

"Sit," she said, following her own order as she gave it. "What brings you here then? You're usually pretty happy for me to keep out of your way."

"I need to tell you something. I don't know if it's linked to this strange situation but it could well be, so..."

The Spitfire Project

Sipping her coffee, Mac indicated that she should continue.

"For the past year, I've been involved in an anarchist organisation in London."

The captain's eyes popped open. She swallowed, then took another drink from her mug.

"Makes sense," she said at last.

"You're not shocked?"

"I'm a little surprised," Mac conceded. "But it had to be something, and anarchism is spreading across this country like a rash right now. It was only a matter of time before they started converting the young and privileged. It makes perfect sense."

"Do you sympathise with the anarchists?" Sola asked, realising she hadn't considered the possibility.

"I sympathise with the experience that made them turn that way, but I find the idea unrealistic and the methods unpalatable."

"The bombings?"

"Yes."

"That wasn't them."

Mac smiled sympathetically at her.

"Yes it was."

She tried to force back the wave of anger that washed over her.

"I don't believe it."

"I'm afraid that doesn't prevent it from being true, Lady Austin. But that's hardly our concern right now."

"What is our concern?"

"Who found out about your little double life, and why did they want to kill you for it?"

"Duke Bernard."

The words were out of her mouth before she'd even thought of them – she hadn't made the connection before, and with everything else she'd even forgotten the mysterious file with her father's name on it.

"Who?"

"Duke Russell Bernard. He found me going through papers in his study, he looked like he was going to attack me. There was this file, it had my father's name…"

At that, Mac sat forward, resting her elbows on the table.

"What was in the file?"

"I didn't understand any of it. It was technical drawings, diagrams..." She could see the captain's shoulders sag in disappointment. "Sorry."

Mac shrugged.

"I assure you it would have meant equally little to me. Those are the times you want someone like Ethan or my father around."

"Your father!" exclaimed Sola.

"What about him?"

"He was an inventor. My father wasn't, so far as I know, I have no reason to think he would have known more about that sort of diagram than I did. But your father would have."

"You think this is the connection?" asked Mac, her eyes lighting up.

"Well it could be," Sola said. "I mean, it's thin, but it's the only thing I've come up with, and I've been thinking about it constantly. You?"

"So have I, and I don't have a better theory."

"Where does that leave us?"

"Do you truly believe this Duke Bernard person is ruthless enough to want to kill you?"

"I would have said no before..."

"But?" the captain prompted.

"He did look murderous that night. And I can't think of anybody else who would want me dead."

"I have to ask... not even the anarchists?"

"No," she said firmly. "I know they were using me, I'm not a complete idiot, but they also counted me as one of them. And even if they didn't, I don't believe I'd worn out my use."

"I like this calculating side of you, Lady Austin," chuckled Mac. "I'll make some enquiries when we're in Glasgow. Thank you for coming to tell me."

Sola nodded. She was about to get up and leave, but then realised she didn't know where to go. She could hardly go back to the workshop, the weather was pretty awful up on deck, and the idea of sitting alone in her room was far from appealing.

"Do you want a game of cards? Keep you away from the books a little longer?"

It was worth it for the captain's face — a strange mix of confusion and surprise.

"Have you and Carlisle had a lover's tiff or something?" she asked.

Her tone was joking, but Sola was sure the stricken look on her face was enough to answer the captain's question.

"I..."

Mac shook her head, silencing Sola with a wave of her hand.

"I honestly don't want to know. A game sounds like an excellent idea."

CHAPTER ELEVEN

A day of fascinating revelations. Sola Austin, an anarchist! Well who'd have thought it. I'm no fan of the ideology, but it's such an entertaining twist on my view of her that I almost don't care. Ethan seems to though. I do hope that sorts itself out soon enough, because I don't know what I'm going to do with the girl if I can't shove her into the workshop.

In real terms, today's news doesn't help me towards knowing what to do, but it does feel good to know even a fraction more about what is going on here. Finding out about this Duke Bernard is on the to-do list for sure. I may do some digging at the trade conference in Glasgow. Someone there is sure to know him, though I'll have to be subtle – maybe I should ask Lady Austin, professional spy, for her expert advice. God, what a strange world it is.

The volume of coffee she'd been drinking probably wasn't helping Mac to sleep, but it did help her get through the day on so little sleep. There was a balance to be struck, but she wasn't getting it yet.

She lay awake thinking about anarchism – specifically, Marcus' horror when he'd found out about the bombings. He'd been ready to throw the group out of his guesthouse, even report them to the police. She had the letter to prove it. Abroad, and unable to contact him with any speed, she'd hung in suspense, with no idea what to do, seeing all the dangers immediately.

In the end, the leader of the group – Jesse Armitage – had given him what he called an ultimatum. Mac called it blackmail. If he kicked them out or reported them, Jesse would also report Marcus for aiding escaped slaves, and for being one himself. Marcus helped too many people to give it up. Besides, she knew he wouldn't leave London until he either died or found his sister. He needed the guesthouse as a cover for his true aims. Mac had a personal interest in it too – without him, the Spitfire wouldn't have Tristan, a child born by a slave who'd been raped by her master and run to the guesthouse, knowing she would find help and safety there.

Anyway, Marcus refused to talk about the bombings now. She could tell he was still cut up with guilt over housing the anarchists. After all, most of the dead were black servants and slaves, the people he was trying to help. She wished she could reassure him that he was doing the right thing, but he wouldn't let her. Besides, who knew if it was the right thing. It was even more morally ambiguous than kidnapping someone to save their life.

She banged her head against the pillow, wishing she would just fall asleep.

By the next morning, Austin was back in the workshop. Mac had no idea if she and Ethan were arguing or kissing, but she expected that if they were arguing they'd resolve it. She consulted her compass and turned the wheel slightly, then glanced up at the crow's nest. Catching Tristan's eye, she beckoned him. He was by her side within thirty seconds, though he still limped across the deck.

"Need something, Captain?"

"You, at full working capacity. You've been up there for five hours now, did you take any water? Food? Have you eaten breakfast? Were you wearing goggles?"

"Alright, Mother."

"*Tristan.*"

He looked guilty. "No, Captain."

"No to what?"

"Everything you just asked."

She rolled her eyes.

"For god's sake, Lynch, I don't think less of you for getting shot, I was shot too! You don't have to prove anything to me. Take a break, eat something, drink something."

"Who's going to cover the crow's nest?" he asked.

She frowned, thinking through the crew. James and Rob were sorting out an oil leak – Ethan had already fixed the pipe, but the mess was a hazard in itself. Henry and Gloria were carrying out an inventory of stock. She sighed. A constant presence in the crow's nest wasn't necessary, but with everything that was happening, it made her feel safer.

"I'll get Ethan to."

"That's cruel, Captain."

She grimaced, feeling guilty.

"He's done it in the past. He'll be fine. He can wear the harness. Just... go get food."

With a weight in the pit of her stomach, she walked with him down to the lower level, and waited until he had disappeared into the galley before knocking on the workshop door.

"Come in."

When she opened the door, it was clear she had interrupted an important conversation, and a fresh wave of guilt washed over her.

"Ethan, I need you to take a shift up in the crow's nest," she said, wanting to look at the ground but forcing herself to keep eye contact.

He swallowed, and she could see the blood drain out of his face.

"I mean, if you want to help take inventory or clear up the oil leak, and can get one of the others to come up onto deck instead..."

He shook his head.

"No, it's fine. I've done it before."

"What's the issue?" said Austin, frowning in confusion.

Ethan blushed. Mac was glad, at least it was getting some blood back into his face.

"I'm pretty terrified of heights," he admitted.

Austin gave him a look of pure disbelief.

"You work on an airship," she stated.

"I'm aware of the irony, Sola."

"He works in a room with no windows," Mac added.

Austin glanced around, as though only just realising it.

"One of the many reasons I can't stand being down here," she said, with a smile to lighten the statement and hide just how true it was. "Come on then. I am sorry, Ethan."

"It's fine."

"Wait," said Austin.

Mac turned back around.

"What?"

"I could do it," she said.

"Sorry?"

"Go up into the crow's nest. I could... I mean, I'm pretty much doing nothing anyway. Ethan could do with a few hours to work without me distracting him... and if he's scared..." she trailed off, and then just repeated, "I could do it."

"Sola, you don't have to..."

She gave him a withering look.

"I'm not scared of heights," she said.

Mac considered the idea. Austin already acted like a member of the crew, would it be so bad to give her a few of the responsibilities that came along with that? Getting up into the crow's nest might be a bit difficult, but once she was up there, it was only boredom that would really cause an issue.

"Rig up the harness, Ethan," she said. "I'm not going through all this just for her to die falling off the rigging."

"Are you seriously going for this, Captain?"

Shrugging, Mac said, "She makes a good argument."

Austin grinned triumphantly.

"*But*," Mac added, "if she can't get up there, I still want you to do it."

Ethan looked slightly shell-shocked, unsure what had just happened.

"Come on then," Mac said again, turning and walking out.

On the deck, Ethan clipped a leather harness onto a complicated pulley system that her father had built for him, so that he could climb on the rigging knowing he wouldn't fall. Unfortunately it hadn't cured his phobia, but it did mean he could get up into the crow's nest if he really had to.

He helped Austin to strap herself into it, and Mac couldn't help smirking at his red face when he apologised profusely for brushing her leg. Austin, to her credit, was laughing.

"So just climb up and into the basket, right Captain?" she said with a grin.

Mac handed her a water skin, and pulled her goggles off her head.

"It's pretty windy when you get up there," she explained. "Stick the water in..." she realised that Austin didn't have a belt.

Luckily, the other girl was way ahead of her, and had tucked it into the loose part at the top of her boot.

"Thanks, Captain Sheridan," she said, smiling grimly at the climb ahead of her.

"The harness is totally secure," said Ethan. "If you lose grip, it'll catch you. Then just feed the ropes through the pulley to get down gently."

"I'm not going to lose my grip, Ethan."

"That's the spirit," laughed Mac. "Go for it, then."

Ethan was almost as white watching Austin climb as he had been at the thought of doing it himself. Mac couldn't deny his concern was sweet, and offered some reassuring words.

"The harness is totally secure, you idiot, you said it yourself. Relax."

She wasn't relaxed herself, however. As she watched, it occurred to her that she should have given Austin her gloves to protect her hands from rope burn.

Since when did you care if she hurt her precious little hands, said a snide voice in the back of her head. *I just don't want to hear her whining about it,* she replied to herself, and then forcefully ended the internal conversation.

Progress was slow, but she was still on the netted part of the rigging, The climb wasn't too challenging at that point, though the wind was obviously throwing her a little. So far, she hadn't faltered, and just continued moving up the ropes, not with total confidence, but with more than Ethan had ever shown.

The first issue came when she had to switch to a different sheet of the rigging, crossing a large gap. Mac marvelled at how something she did at least once a day now seemed so nerve-wracking, and was even more surprised to find she *wanted* Austin to make it to the top.

Austin shuffled sideways to the edge of the net she was on, and then let go with one hand, stretching it out to the side. Her fingertips were an inch away from the other rope. She brought the hand back to hold onto the rigging.

The ropes were swaying a little in the wind, and she decided to make use of it. When she swayed to the side, she stretched out a leg and hooked her foot around the rope. She used her legs to pull the two areas of rigging closer to each other, and then neatly stepped across, as though she were on the ground.

"I'm impressed," Mac admitted to Ethan, who looked like he was going to vomit.

Austin continued to progress up the other sheet of rigging, eventually reaching the metal balloon. Mac tensed. This was the hardest part of the whole climb. Austin obviously realised it. Her progress slowed even further, she flattened herself to the metal and gripped onto the ropes as best she could (it was impossible to get your hands around them when they were flat on the balloon, Mac knew). Then she slipped. The harness caught her, but Mac's heart beat hard in her chest all the same. Ethan had shut his eyes.

She looked back up at Austin, wondering whether she would use the harness to descend. Somehow, she guessed not. To her pleasure, Sola swung back in toward the rigging and began to climb again. This time, when she reached the balloon, she virtually stopped. She moved so slowly it was almost impossible to see, but eventually she reached the top.

"Don't stand up," Mac whispered.

She could feel Ethan's eyes on her, confused, no doubt, by her concern, and ignored him. This was the part where she tended to walk in a crouch, but Austin went one step further, crawling along the metal. It wasn't elegant, but it did the trick. She reached the nest, grabbed onto it, and clambered inside.

Mac grinned.

"Looks like you should go back to work, Ethan," she said.

He nodded, and then smiled. She could see the pride shining out of his eyes.

"She's growing on you then, Captain?" he said, raising his eyebrows.

"If she's going to insist on being useful, she may well," said Mac, refusing to elaborate. "I hope you realise she's shown *you* up quite considerably. Go do what you're good at. Don't worry, I'll keep an eye."

"Thanks, Captain."

When he'd left, Mac climbed back up to the wheel and altered their bearing. She glanced at the crow's nest, to see blonde hair flying around in the wind. Smiling to herself, she consulted her compass once again.

CHAPTER TWELVE

I don't think my body has ever hurt this much. Muscles I didn't even know I had are aching. Now I have tried climbing the rigging, I have a whole new appreciation for the ease with which Tristan does it. Hell, the whole crew is capable of clambering up and down, and they don't seem to limp afterwards. Other than Ethan of course. I have never seen him climb, and now I know why. He's scared of heights. It seems a very odd plight for someone who works on an airship, and when I asked him, he said he had done it for the opportunity to learn from Patrick Sheridan.

I can't help wondering if now, with Patrick Sheridan dead, he would ever consider leaving this life and moving on to university. I don't want to ask, because if the idea isn't in his head, I wouldn't like to put it there. I certainly hope he will be on the Spitfire for as long as I am. I wondered if our friendship was over after his reaction to the anarchism argument. We've both just been ignoring it, however, and haven't spoken about it since. I don't know if that's the best way to deal with the situation, but it will do for now.

I hope I will be allowed to help on the ship again. More and more, I am able to see why this lifestyle appeals to so many people. For one, I know I will get a good sleep tonight.

Sola woke with the sun on her face. For once, instead of going straight down to the galley and the workshop, she took the staircase up instead, heading out onto the deck. Henry was steering, and Tristan was swinging around the ropes, laughing at James, who was trying to follow. The sight made her smile, as well as reminding her of the agony her legs had been in climbing the stairs.

The day was mild, and relatively calm, so she stayed on the deck, going to speak with Henry at the wheel.

"Sleep well?" she asked.

"Yeah, up at four though," he replied.

"Why so early?"

He shrugged. She had noticed that Henry wasn't exactly the most talkative fellow, though he'd never been unfriendly and was always up for a card game in the lounge. Sola glanced around, looking at the horizon, then back down at the deck.

"Henry?"

"Yeah?"

"Is that a staircase?"

He glanced around to the back of the deck.

"Yup. Goes onto the back balcony. We don't go down there much."

"Could I?"

He shrugged again. Rolling her eyes at the lack of communication, Sola descended the spiral steps, thrilled that there was a part of the ship she hadn't yet discovered. The back balcony was exactly what it sounded like, a stretch of decking along the back of the strip with a railing. She was just admiring the view when she heard someone behind her.

"Good morning, Lady Austin."

She turned around to see Captain Sheridan, standing in a doorway that led to her study. For some reason, she felt as though she'd been caught doing something she shouldn't.

"Good morning, Captain Sheridan," she said, determined to fight that feeling.

"I don't usually find anyone else here," said the captain, stepping outside and closing the door behind her.

"Is that a ship rule?" asked Sola.

"No," she said, smiling. "The crew just knows I do a lot of my thinking here."

"I can see why," Sola said. "It's very peaceful."

"It is that. How did you find your way to it?"

"Henry said I could go down. I think he wanted me out of his way."

"Yes, he has been in a bit of a mood recently," mused Mac. "I'll have to ask soon if he doesn't pull out of it."

"I hadn't noticed."

The captain shrugged.

"It's not your job to. How are you feeling after yesterday?" she asked, smirking.

"I'm fine," said Sola, not wanting to admit to her pain.

"Keep walking around a lot," Mac said, laughing. "It'll help, even if it hurts like a bastard."

"It doesn't hurt."

"Liar. It's unusual for you not to be in the workshop by now," observed Mac.

"It's a nice day," Sola said.

"Nothing to do with your spat with Carlisle?"

"I thought you didn't want to know."

"I don't. But I thought you guys had sorted it out between the two of you."

Sola turned to look out at the horizon again, resting her arms on the railing.

"We haven't exactly spoken about it."

"I suggest you do. He's a reasonable man, he just has a distaste for violence and he doesn't like the thought of you having been in danger. That's why he was angry, really."

"Thanks," said Sola, hoping to close the conversation.

Sheridan took the point.

"Well, I have plenty to do. I'll leave you to do *your* thinking."

She disappeared back through the door. The thought of bringing up the argument with Ethan when they'd both silently agreed not made her nervous. But maybe it was the best thing to do, if she wanted to honestly get past it.

With a grimace at the thought of the pain it would cause her, Sola began to climb back up the stairs.

In the workshop, Ethan was hard at work, and as usual, Sola wasn't entirely sure what he was working on, but it looked very complex. She pulled a chair up to him, and waited until she had his attention.

"Morning, Sola," he said, pushing his goggles up onto his head.

"I think we should talk, Ethan," she opened, afraid she would back out if she left it too long.

"That sounds serious. What about?"

"I think you know."

"Ah."

She tucked her hair behind her ear.

"I just don't want it between us the whole time. I'd like to explain myself."

"Go on then."

"Erm," she coughed. "I met the leader of the group at a party. We got on brilliantly. He gave me an address, and I decided to go see him there. Except when I got there, it wasn't just him, it was a whole group of people, who were extraordinarily welcoming. And they had these heartbreaking stories - about workhouses, and slavery, and all sorts of awful things. What is the point of a government that doesn't protect its people at all, Ethan?"

"I'm not denying problems in the government, Sola, but the anarchists are hardly better, for god's sake."

"I don't know about that. But I honestly felt they were good people trying to do a good thing, and they made me feel like one of them. Maybe I was naive, maybe I was just plain wrong, but I can't bear you judging me for it. I was trying to do a good thing. I certainly didn't kill anyone!"

Ethan sighed.

"I'm not judging you… and I know you didn't kill people. Just the thought of it. What could have happened to you - what would have, if we hadn't gotten you!"

"My life has been under more threat on board this ship than it ever was in London," she replied sharply, images of the pirate attack leaping into her brain.

"Do you honestly believe that?"

She went to answer, but then she remembered the file with her father's name, the look in Duke Bernard's eyes, and how scared she had been to go to his for dinner on the night of her kidnap.

"Maybe. I don't know. I've certainly felt the danger more.

Ignorance is bliss, I guess."

"So long as it doesn't get you killed, it is."

"What do you want from me? I'm here, I'm fine."

"That's all I want from you," he said seriously.

She smiled at the implication.

"Good. Are we fine, then?"

"Of course we are. And Sola?"

"Yes?"

"Thanks for the crow's nest yesterday," he said, smiling.

"No problem at all. It was fun."

He laughed loudly.

"Even those who aren't scared of heights tend to classify it as 'boring as hell'," he explained.

"I suppose it could be dull if you did it a lot," she admitted.

"Do you want to do it a lot?"

Sola groaned.

"With the way my body's feeling today? Not especially. But when I see Tristan and James chasing each other around the rigging like they are this morning… I'd love to have that ability."

"So would I," said Ethan. "I think you're far more likely to achieve it though. Just be careful."

"I think I'll stick to the harness for now."

"For my sake, please do."

"Your sake?" she said, raising her eyebrows.

"Ask Mac, I just about threw up when you slipped yesterday."

"You know, that could have been romantic if you hadn't mentioned vomiting," she teased.

He grinned.

"Can I get a second chance at that sentence?"

"Sure, go for it."

He stood, placing his hand dramatically over his heart.

"Sola, when you slipped yesterday, my heart stopped beating."

She laughed, and slipped her arms around his neck, then, before she had a chance to think about it, pressed her lips to his. He froze for a second, and then wrapped his hands around her waist, pulling her closer to him. Any doubts she had melted away. She pulled back after a while, resting her forehead against his.

"We waited far too long to do that," she said.

"Couldn't agree more."

"Shall we make up for lost time?"

"Absolutely."

By lunch, as much as she enjoyed kissing him, Sola was feeling a little guilty for keeping Ethan from his work. So, despite his complaints, she left him in the workshop. She headed upstairs into the crew lounge, unable to wipe the broad grin from her face. Captain Sheridan was sitting at the smaller table, with brown leather and a large needle. She looked up, then starting laughing.

"Am I to assume Ethan will get nothing done today?" she asked.

Sola squirmed uncomfortably.

"I've left him to work now."

"I doubt he'll be focusing on clockwork or steam," Mac teased further.

"Shut up."

"Lunch is sitting on the table if you want any."

On the large dining table was a large pot of soup, with bowls and spoons beside it. Sola ladled some into a bowl, mostly to avoid Mac's amused gaze. But feeling it would be rude to sit at a different table, when there was no one else in the room, she sat opposite the captain.

"What are you working on?"

"A belt."

Sola glanced at Mac's waist, confirming that the wide utility belt was still there.

"You need another?"

"No, this one is fine."

Sola blew on her soup.

"I don't understand."

"Lady Austin, what does every member of my crew have?"

"A belt?" Sola guessed, though in reality she had never noticed.

"A belt. MacKinnon wears two for god's sake."

"They already have them, then," Sola said, still confused.

"Lady Austin, have your experiences yesterday put you off airship work for good?" asked Mac pointedly.

"No!" Sola insisted immediately. "I'd love to do some more... oh."

"And it clicks," said Mac, turning back to the material.

"You don't have to do that."

"If you're going to learn, you may as well have the tools. We'll look into getting you a weapon in Glasgow, and I'll teach you with mine in the meantime."

"Are you serious?"

"I suppose it's not a bad idea for you to know how to defend yourself, if you're as endangered as my father believed you were."

"It's not as exciting when you put it that way," said Sola grimly.

"The best part about guns is when you don't have to use them," Mac agreed. "And by the way, giving you a gun is not a way of saying, 'feel free to come up on deck if we're attacked by pirates'."

Sola shuddered at the memory.

"You don't need to worry about that, believe me."

"Not even if Ethan's on deck?"

She was silent.

"Exactly. Come on, we'll get some practice off the back balcony."

They took the route through Mac's study, and once they were out, she took a gun with a large circular barrel and passed it to Sola. It was reassuringly solid.

"What am I to aim for?"

"Aim to not fall down when you fire it," Mac replied.

Sola braced herself, pointing the gun out into the sky, and squeezed the trigger. The impact sent shock waves up her arms, which were already aching from the previous day's exertions.

"Ow!"

"Well, you didn't fall," said Mac, grinning. "Try again, you'll get used to it."

Mac pulled out another weapon from her hip, a daintier, slimmer piece. She fired it, frowned, and stuck it back inside her belt.

"Problem?"

The captain shook her head.

"My father's gun," she explained. "I don't have the hang of it yet – not sure I'll get it, honestly. Go on, try again."

Sola fired again and again until she'd emptied the gun of bullets. Every shot hurt, but she did learn to anticipate the pain and brace herself for it.

"That'll do for today. We'll have to use the deck for target practice, but I won't make you do it in front of the crew until I'm sure you won't embarrass yourself."

"I appreciate it."

"Go find Ethan. I doubt he's being productive anyway, you guys may as well be enjoying yourselves."

Sola blushed.

"Thanks, Captain."

She ducked through into the study. When the door swung shut behind her, leaving Mac on the back balcony, she stopped. Curiosity swept through her. This was Sheridan's study and bedroom. Who knew what she could find in here? But if the captain came back in... they were just starting to be able to stand each other...

Quickly, she walked over to the bookshelf. One of the volumes was clearly a photograph album, and she selected that one. The photos were largely of the Spitfire - Mac, her father, and the crew (with several members she didn't recognise) over the years. On the last page, however, was a picture of Mac, not much younger than she now was, and beside her was a man with his arm slung over her shoulders. A tall, black man that Sola recognised as Marcus Tate, the owner of the anarchist's guesthouse.

CHAPTER THIRTEEN

Arrived in Glasgow early this morning. Not looking forward to the utter pointless ego-fest of the trade conference this evening, but what can you do? Also not wild about leaving the ship, and Sola Austin, for such a long period, but I do have other duties now (though I frequently wish I did not).

Shooting lessons with Austin are going relatively well, although she continues to pull considerably to the left. Must look into getting her a gun while I am here, though it will have to wait until tomorrow. Austin and Ethan's relationship continues, though the most I see of it is loving looks across the crew lounge. I have no idea whether they've taken it to the bedroom yet, and no desire to think about it (damn Riddle for putting the thought in my head last night). Disturbing, as that is the bed where Marcus and I… anyway.

Speaking of Riddle, he has requested land leave for these two days in Glasgow. Apparently it is only fair as "Rob got Bristol". The man acts like a child. Nevertheless, I have granted it. Hopefully he will not be as fixated on Ethan's sex life if he returns to having one of his own.

As she had in London, Mac enjoyed the relative emptiness of the Spitfire that day. Gloria and Rob were aboard, but Henry had disappeared off to do something in the city, Ethan and Sola were out (as she'd promised they could be), James was on leave, and Tristan, after helping to unload cargo, had gone to join him for a few hours.

She took the time to inspect the ship without any interruptions, making a list of everything that needed to be fixed, which she then dropped off in Ethan's workshop. She still struggled not to think of it as her father's workshop. Early on, she had learnt to leave him alone when he was working there, not because he wanted her to, but because it was where he was at his most unintelligible. If it wasn't his inventions he was talking about, it was philosophy, and both meant absolutely nothing to her. Maybe she should have tried harder. Maybe if she had, she would have known him better. Maybe he'd have mentioned George and Beatrice Austin, and she'd be able to sort this mess out. But she hadn't, and now he was dead. She left the workshop.

Rob wasn't keen to leave the Spitfire, despite Glasgow being his home city. On the basis that everyone deserved privacy, Mac didn't ask why. She went into the city in the afternoon, to organise for more provisions to be loaded onto the Spitfire, and ate lunch in town, amazed by how long it had been since she'd eaten non-ship food. Then she posted a letter to Marcus and picked up a newspaper, before heading back home.

The front page was all about the trade conference. It was a sickeningly glowing review of Edward Bingley and all that he had done to 'unite the shipping industry, without the need for the disruptiveness of trade unions' - a an unsubtle jab at the postal strike that had caused so much havoc. She wondered whether Bingley himself had paid the paper for the piece, or if it was the government in his pocket that had done so. Snorting, she left the paper on a table in the lounge and went to bath.

Mac dressed for the evening with care - she wasn't often required to look formal. She wore a crisp white shirt and black trousers, with her only pair of leather boots that hadn't been scuffed endlessly. As a last minute decision, she chose a red waistcoat to match the jacket Tamsin had given her. Leaving off the utility belt was a wrench, but it wouldn't exactly show a spirit of co-operation and unity to turn up with a gun on her hip.

She didn't want to leave early, so she stopped by the lounge, envious of the relaxed dinner they were eating together. That said, Henry didn't look relaxed at all. She was beginning to genuinely worry about him.

Rob wolf-whistled when he saw her.

"You going out somewhere, Captain?" said Tristan cheekily.

"Keep on like that and I'll send you in my place," she said darkly.

"I don't think Edward Bingley would much like that," laughed Gloria.

"Edward Bingley can take what he doesn't like and shove it up his arse," Mac responded with a scowl. "I hate jumping through his fucking hoops."

"What's wrong with Edward Bingley?" asked Austin.

"Bingley's shipping?" said Mac, wondering if she knew who they were talking about.

"So?" was the reply, indicating she did.

"As in, the largest importer of opium in Britain?"

"No way."

"Afraid so," said Tristan. "Not to mention half the government in his back pocket."

"How the hell do you know this stuff?"

The crew laughed.

"It's like when everyone knows Lord Someone is having an affair with Lady Someone Else but nobody actually ever talks about in public," Mac explained.

Austin frowned.

"My family use Bingley's," she said.

"Well then, you are funding Britain's opiate addiction," Mac said lightly. "But you didn't know. Obviously it's only a well-known thing in lower circles."

"And of course the highest circles of all," chimed in Tristan again.

"Exactly. And now I have to look him in the eye and enjoy being bathed by the shining golden light of his glory. As you can imagine, I eagerly anticipate it," she paused, allowing them to laugh at her expense. "Have a better evening than I'm about to, folks."

The event was always going to be unpleasant, for a variety of reasons, but there was one that she'd actually almost forgotten about. Quite simply, everyone was going to insist on giving her their condolences. It felt like so long had passed since her father died, but it had only been a little over a month, and most captains who knew and respected him were still reeling from it. She was shaking the hand of the fifth or sixth, when someone behind her put a hand on her shoulder.

"Hello *Captain*," a familiar voice said in her ear.

She whirled around.

"Helena!"

"My condolences also," said the woman, with a sympathetic smile. "But I mustn't forget to give you my congratulations. You may now join the ranks of the much maligned female airship captains."

She couldn't help laughing.

"I haven't found most people too bad, actually. I'm beginning to think you've been exaggerating all these years."

"Oh it's not *most people* that are the issue. It's the ranks of male airship captains who feel as though we somehow threaten their masculinity," she giggled, and added in a stage whisper, "if they need their job to be masculine, is all I'm saying…"

Mac grinned. It was almost worth going through the whole charade to see Helena again. They'd met at another of these events when Mac was twelve and despite the ten-year age gap become fast friends.

They headed into the hall together, taking seats next to each other at one of the many round tables that were scattered across the room. Most were still mingling, and Mac knew she really should be forging connections, but she couldn't resist the chance to catch up with an old friend.

"This is the sisterhood then," said a blonde man in his fifties, sitting in the chair next to Mac. "Nice to see our womanly counterparts bonding."

"I don't know what you mean by counterparts, Edward, when was the last time you actually worked on an airship?" responded Helena smoothly.

Mac had to bite her cheek to keep from laughing, though Edward Bingley just smiled.

"Your tongue's so sharp it cuts your cheeks, Helena," he replied.

"So long as it cuts other people too," she responded sweetly.

He laughed, and picked up some glasses of champagne from a waiter, passing one to each of them.

"I'll catch up with the two of you after dinner," he said. "Captain Sheridan - my condolences on your loss. Your father was a brilliant man."

"Thank you, Mr Bingley, he certainly was."

Once he was out of the way, Helena jabbed Mac's arm.

"*You* left me hanging *completely* there, traitor."

"Yes, because Edward Bingley is an enemy I want to make in my second month as captain."

"Hmm. I suppose I'll let you off. But by the time we have another one of these…"

"Deal," she agreed.

Conversation ran from crew to trade to ships. After an hour, Mac relaxed into it, and for the first time, felt truly at ease as the captain of the Spitfire, not as though she were just pretending or playing at it while her father was holed up in his workshop. Dinner was served, and she ate, glad of the chance to rest her throat after a particularly heated discussion on trading from Asia. A couple of the captains already had, and Mac was equal parts jealous and relieved that it wasn't her. Their stories made the continent sound incredible, but even legitimately trading from there would make Edward Bingley see them as a threat to his company, and everyone could do without that. She promised herself that if Bingley's ever collapsed (or maybe just if Edward himself died, and someone less slimy took over), she would take the Spitfire further afield than Europe.

After the starter, the man of the hour stood and tapped his fork against his glass. With an inaudible groan, Mac turned to listen to his toast.

"I want to start by thanking all of you for coming today," he began. "The shipping industry has every right to be proud of the unity and co-operation that forms the bedrock of its success. In this era, airships have never been more important. They are the fastest, most comfortable form of transport, and the key to unlocking international trade. Britain can no longer stand in splendid isolation - and neither should we. Which is why today I announce that I will pay an exceptionally generous salary to any captain willing to fly under the flag of Bingley's. The money is good, and the opportunities are even better. Enjoy your dinner and consider your options, and find me afterwards if you are interested in my offer. Thank you again for your presence today."

There was a slightly shell-shocked round of applause.

"Well what do you think of that?" Mac murmured to Helena.

"I think every airship in financial difficulty doesn't have a choice."

Mac stopped in horror.

"Helena, please tell me you aren't in financial difficulty."

"No!" said Helena, horrified. "And I'd rather go bankrupt than work for bloody Edward Bingley. Honestly Mac, I should shoot you just for that."

"Sorry, sorry," she said, grinning in relief. "I hope the other captains have your morals."

"Yes, but you know most of them don't."

She grimaced.

"True enough. Just another step in Bingley's attempt to take over the world then."

"He could have just sent out a telegram and saved us the journey," laughed Helena. "It's far from shocking."

"No, just soul-destroying," sighed Mac, taking a gulp of the so-far untouched champagne.

There was a strange buzzing noise, Mac looked around to see where it was coming from, but saw nothing.

"Mac?" she heard Helena say, though the buzzing got louder.

"Yes, sorry?"

"Mac, are you alright?"

Helena voice was getting quieter and quieter, and her vision was beginning to blur. Mac tried to stand, but stumbled and fell to the ground. She could barely make out Helena's panicked tone as the world went black.

CHAPTER FOURTEEN

Going out with Ethan today was wonderful. Glasgow is a beautiful city, and to be off the Spitfire made a nice change, as much as I do love it. We went for a coffee and looked around the shopping area. I considered just buying a belt (all that money I have from beating James at cards), but the one Mac is making for me is taking shape nicely, and Ethan told me that Mac has made belts for every member of the crew, so I like the gesture. I did buy a large earring, which hooks over the back of my ear and then dangles from the piercing. It is a style I have noticed many of the female airship workers have adopted (there are so many in the city right now! It must be the conference). I also invested in a few books. It has been a while since I read, and while I am sure the captain would lend me some of hers, I don't feel we are quite at the stage where I am willing to ask her. Further, a hairbrush! At last, an end to trying to comb this mess with my fingers. Getting all the knots out was painful, but worth it.

According to the crew, Edward Bingley uses his business as a front for opium smuggling, and the government is well aware of it. With everything I heard from the anarchists, this news is hardly shocking, but it does horrify me that I wasn't aware of it before. How much else goes on that I have no idea of, I must wonder. I don't envy Mac having to make nice with him tonight - she certainly didn't appear to be looking forward to it.

After a casual game of cards in the lounge, I retired early to my room. It has been a lovely day.

So far, there had been no click in the lock to indicate she was trapped for the night. Sola wondered whether they now trusted her not to try to escape, which brought up the awkward question - if she could, would she? The answer was most likely not. She now believed in this mysterious danger against her, and could think of worse places to keep safe than the Spitfire. But she couldn't help marveling at how much had changed in such a short time. Ethan had said he couldn't imagine her getting married and settling down - well, neither could she. But a month ago she thought she would escape that fate through Jesse and the anarchists. Now she had no doubt that she wanted to take to the skies.

    She smiled and stood up from the vanity table, closing over her journal. It was late, but the crew had indicated Captain Sheridan wouldn't be back until gone midnight. She wondered how it was going. No matter how smart the captain had looked, or how coldly polite she had been to Sola at the start of her time on the Spitfire, it was difficult to imagine Mac fitting in a formal dinner setting. Chuckling at the image, she looked toward the bed. In honesty, she wasn't tired yet. She'd left the lounge because she wanted to write up her journal and have some peace and quiet, but she didn't want to sleep. Immediately, the thought of the back balcony came to mind. She stepped out into the corridor and tried the door to Mac's study, but it was locked. As quietly as she could, she climbed the stairs up onto the deck. Which was when she saw the rigging. What better time to practice? Ethan never let her climb without the harness, and though she understood why, she felt it was time to progress. Tentatively, she gripped the rope and began to climb. She reached the top of the first stretch, and didn't yet dare try the gap unaided. Carefully, slowly, she turned around to sit on the rope, twisting her hands into it to ensure she wouldn't fall.

    Glasgow looked incredible at night, buildings silhouetted by the amber light from the street-lamps. But when she focused her eyes nearer to her, she saw shadowy figures on the dock. They were conversing in whispers, and she couldn't make out what they were saying. She tried to stay perfectly still and silent. It could be harmless, but her instincts were telling her it wasn't. She watched as they approached the Spitfire, passing by other ships until there was nowhere else they could be going. She had to warn the crew. But if she tried to get down now, they'd see her, no doubt. And it was probably her they wanted. She was completely defenseless. All Sola could do was watch as they climbed the ramp up onto the deck, and slipped inside the door. As soon as they disappeared she began to climb. She had to try not to rush, to be

The Spitfire Project

careful, but it was difficult. Once she was down, she ran onto the upper deck and down the stairs to the back balcony, praying that her suspicions would be right. Holding her breath, she tried the door into Mac's study. It swung open. Inside the room, she glanced around, relieved to almost immediately see Mac's utility belt, with one of her guns still in it. She grabbed the weapon and made sure it was loaded.

Then she heard the first shots. She desperately tried the door into the corridor, but it held firmly shut. She ran back up onto the main deck, and threw herself in the door and down the stairs. She rushed down the second flight, into Ethan's workshop. The first thing she saw was a broad man pointing a gun, and she fired without thinking. The force of it threw her back, but the man crumpled and fell to the ground. Behind him stood Ethan.

"Sola, oh my god…"

She ran to him and pulled him into her arms.

"What's going on? I was on deck and they came, they're here for me, I'm sure of it."

He stepped out of her embrace and walked over to the door, which he locked.

"What about the others?" she said.

"They can defend themselves. My priority is to look after you."

"Last I checked, I was looking after you," she said, looking grimly at the body on the ground.

"Thanks for that," he replied, "but we're still staying down here. Mac would kill me if I did anything else."

They stood in silence, listening to the shots and scuffles on the floor above. Even when they eventually stopped, neither of them moved until there was a knock at the door.

"Ethan!" yelled Gloria. "Are you alright? Have you seen Sola? She's not in her room!"

"I'm in here!" Sola called back. "We're both fine!" She unlocked the door. "Everyone else?"

"Alive, and mostly fine. A little battered. I don't think they counted on us being armed and ready to fire at a moment's notice," she said grimly. "We were just worried about you. Were you down here the whole time?"

"No, I was up on deck at first. I saw them, but they didn't see me."

"On deck?" asked Gloria, sounding confused.

"I just wanted a little fresh air," she explained, feeling a little guilty.

"I thought Henry had locked up," said Gloria, shrugging.

"Maybe he was waiting till Captain Sheridan got back?"

"No… she was going to come in through the back balcony, so he could lock everything else." Gloria frowned. "The idiot probably just forgot. Is that a body behind you?"

Sola was surprised it had taken her so long to notice.

"I came down and he was about to shoot Etha…"

Gloria's eyebrows shot up.

"You killed him?"

Put that starkly, Sola was shocked herself. First she was climbing rigging and learning to shoot; now she had actually killed somebody.

"Yeah… yes. I did."

Gloria nodded, impressed.

"Nice shooting. Let's get him onto the dock, that's where we're dumping the others."

They wouldn't let Sola help with the bodies, a decision she didn't protest. Instead she went through to the galley and begun to cook. It had always relaxed her, and she was good at it. She hadn't offered to join the cooking rota on the Spitfire yet, but it was part of her plan to show she could be useful, and now seemed as good a time as any.

Halfway through making the meal, she felt the airship begin to move. Leaving the stew on the hob, she ran out, bumping into Ethan in the hall.

"What the fuck is going on?

"Captain's orders," he said. "If something happened, leave Glasgow immediately and regroup in Inverness."

"She expected this was going to happen?"

"That would be putting it a little strongly. She anticipated something might happen, and planned accordingly."

"So we're going to Inverness."

"Pretty much."

Sola rolled her eyes. She thought she was getting closer to being involved on the Spitfire, but evidently many discussions were still way above her head.

"Well, I'm cooking. Dinner will be ready in half an hour."

"You can cook?"

"There's no need to sound so shocked, Mr Carlisle."

"I didn't think the aristocracy did their own cooking," he teased.

"I had someone teach me," she said primly, thinking with fondness of her aunt's maid, who had gone behind Judith's back to do so. Who had known the skill would end up so useful?

"Well aren't you just pitching in perfectly," teased Ethan. "Don't worry about Mac. She'll head up to Inverness and be back to getting on your nerves in no time."

"And James?"

He looked less certain at that.

"Hopefully. If she finds him, or he hears what's happened from someone else."

Sola looked down.

"This just keeps getting worse and worse, doesn't it?"

"It's not brilliant," Ethan agreed, stepping in to hug her.

She wrapped her arms around his neck and rested her head on his chest.

"It's a miracle we're all still alive," she whispered.

"Maybe. But we *are*."

She pulled away and smiled.

"I suppose we are. I'll see you in the lounge for dinner?"

"Sure. Go be chef."

"When you've eaten the best stew of your life, I am going to force you to take back every snide, sarcastic comment you've just made."

He grinned and quickly kissed her.

"I'll make it up to you somehow."

CHAPTER FIFTEEN

God knows what happened to Mac last night. One moment she was fine – we were grumbling about Edward Bingley, as you do – and the next she was spacing out and then it looked as though she was having some sort of fit.

I got her out as soon as possible and took her back to the Empress. Rare good fortune that Dr. Stephenson has been travelling with us. He treated her and says she should be fine, but his grim assessment of the situation is that she was poisoned. How, and by who, and why? I hope the girl hasn't gotten herself involved with anything stupid.

Helena heard a noise behind her and turned to see that Mac was sitting up.

"What happened?" she asked groggily.

"Apparently someone wants you dead," Helena replied airily. "You were poisoned. I saved your life, by the way, so now you owe me an eternity of servitude."

"Who poisoned me?" Mac said, brushing aside the jokes.

"I was rather hoping you'd have the answer to that part."

Mac shook her head, frowning.

"I remember... Bingley's toast. And then... nothing."

"The champagne!" gasped Helena, the pieces falling into place. "Jesus, you needn't have worried about making an enemy of Edward Bingley, it looks like you already have."

"Huh?"

"Oh hurry up, Mac! It happened after you drank the champagne, which was given to you by...?"

"Shit."

"At last," she said. "Now the question is why?"

"Yes. But first I need to get back to the Spitfire."

Helena winced.

"Bad news there, Mac. They've taken off. I went to look for Henry, let him know you were safe, but... gone. According to the dock-keepers she was never there, but I saw her yesterday."

Mac blinked several times.

"Inverness," she said.

"Excuse me?"

"They've gone to Inverness. I need to get there. As soon as possible."

Helena frowned.

"I need to be in the city one more day, but then I can make a detour to take you to Inverness, I suppose."

Mac shook her head urgently, and pulled herself out of bed.

"I won't have you involved in this, Helena. It's even more dangerous than I thought it was. Where are my shoes?"

Helena looked at the other captain, astounded by how much she had grown and changed in the single year since they'd last seen each other. Something about Mac's eyes told her there would be no point insisting, or asking for any more information, or saying anything other than...

"Just outside the door. Your jacket's there too."

"Thank you. I owe you, Helena," she smiled grimly. "I don't know about eternal servitude, but we'll meet in the middle somewhere."

"Take care, Captain Sheridan."

Mac acknowledged her with a nod of the head.

"And yourself, Captain Jenson."

"I always do."

CHAPTER SIXTEEN

I confess, a while ago I thought that the mood on the Spitfire would be better if Captain Sheridan weren't around. I couldn't have been more wrong. Henry has barely spoken. His mood is obviously both worrying Gloria and getting on her nerves immensely. Rob and Tristan without James is a strange combination – like 'see no evil' and 'hear no evil' without 'speak no evil', now there is a sculpture nobody has ever made. Ethan tries to put on a good face for me, but I can tell he's worried, as am I. It is plain wrong for an airship to be without its captain. I know we are the ones who left her, but I can't help being scared that something has happened – that we will reach Inverness, and wait there for five days, as was apparently agreed, and still Captain Sheridan will not appear.

Sola glanced to the left at her bed. Ethan was still fast asleep, his dark hair splayed over the pillow. It was natural for them to turn to physical comfort in times like this, she supposed, although she did wonder if it was a good reason to take somebody to bed. Nevertheless... a blush rose to her cheeks as she thought of it. She had no regrets. Not knowing how to word her thoughts on the matter, she chose to not yet write about it. Although she wanted her journal to be an accurate reflection on her life, there were some parts that should be put right, or not at all.

She left him sleeping and joined Rob and Tristan up on deck. They passed over Edinburgh, but didn't stop, so all she got was an aerial view of the city.

"When do you think we'll get to Inverness?"

"Probably midday tomorrow," said Tristan. "It's when will the captain get there that's really the issue."

"By now she'll know the ship's gone," Rob said. "So she knows she has about a week to get to Inverness. I expect she'll get a lift on an airship going that way."

"And if she doesn't make it?"

The two of them glanced at each other.

"Henry'll take over permanently," Tristan said.

"Why didn't that happen in the first place?" asked Sola. "I mean, isn't it normal that a first mate becomes captain if the captain dies?"

Rob laughed.

"Yes, usually. But Henry doesn't want to be captain, really. And we all knew the job would be Mac's some day, though we didn't think it would be so soon."

"Besides," said Tristan, "tradition."

"How so?"

"Oh this is a good story," Rob smiled. "Patrick Sheridan was a university student, struggling with being about twenty times smarter than his lecturers."

"Aislin Mackenzie was a farm-girl who'd moved to the city, searching for work aboard airships. Owning her own airship was her dream. But the industry was even more anti-women then than it is now, and she had no luck," Tristan continued.

"So one rainy day, the two met..." Rob said dramatically.

"How do you know it was rainy?" Tristan asked.

"It was Ireland, I'm guessing. Let me get on with the story. They met, fell wildly in love, and so on. Patrick dropped out of university and persuaded an old airship captain to give the two of them jobs aboard his little ship. Now he was an efficient enough worker, but the whole thing was Aislin's dream, and she was the one who had the passion for it. The old captain came to love her as his own daughter, and in fact offered to marry the two of them aboard the ship, but Aislin objected to being 'owned' by a man, and Patrick didn't mind one way or the other, so long as he had her. Anyway, in his will, the captain left the ship to Aislin, to the shock and horror of the crew. But since she was the captain then, she just fired them all, and she and Patrick hired a new crew of their own. So the first person in Mac's family to captain the

Spitfire wasn't her father – it was her mother."

"And she's named after her mother's surname?"

"Yeah, well, Patrick Sheridan always was a strange guy," said Tristan. "Brilliant, but barking mad."

She laughed.

"I suppose it means I got 'Aislin'."

"What?"

"Aislin. It's my middle name."

The two men looked at her in shock.

"After Mac's mother?"

Too late, Sola remembered that the crew hadn't been included in their revelations about their parents. She summarised the situation quickly for them, leaving them slightly awe-struck.

"It makes sense," said Rob, after he'd absorbed it. "I mean, Captain Sheridan the former did care about you for some reason."

"How did he die?" she asked.

She'd held back for so long, knowing it would be a sensitive area, but now, without Mac around, she couldn't resist any longer.

"Pirate attack," said Tristan.

"Not according to him," corrected Rob. "We were attacked, and we fought back, and he was shot When we'd managed to get away from the 'pirates' he was already virtually dead. He had about enough time left to insist it wasn't a pirate attack, and make Mac promise to save your life."

"And get us into this whole mess," Sola couldn't resist saying.

"I guess we'll just have to hope his daughter can get us out of it," Tristan replied.

"You think she can?"

He smiled.

"If anybody can, it's Mac."

Sola was amazed by the level of loyalty the crew was showing to the captain, even in her absence.

"I think she might need some help. Which is why I wanted to ask you something."

She was regretting the request just ten minutes later, as she clung for dear life onto the ropes of the rigging, flailing with her feet for a grip that wasn't there.

"Come on," said Tristan beside her, annoyingly calm as he hung casually from a rope with only one hand. "Stretch."

"I'm trying to *fucking* stretch," she hissed back.

But she forced herself to relax and hang still form the rope. Taking a deep breath and trying to ignore the pain in her arms and the drop below her, she stretched a foot back, and breathed a sigh of relief when it brushed a rope. She hooked her food around it and pulled it closer; glad to see it was a whole sheet of netted rigging. Carefully, she transferred one hand, and then the other, and swung back on it. Tristan grinned and moved along the rope he was on by placing one hand in front of the other. He swung back and forward a few times to gather momentum, and then let go, flying forward towards the rigging, which he grabbed deftly.

"Showoff," Sola muttered."

He laughed.

"That was good!"

"I think I just about had a heart attack."

"There's no danger," he insisted. "I'd have caught you if it went wrong."

Somehow, she didn't doubt that he would have been capable of it.

"Okay, boss, what's next?" she said, setting her jaw.

"Keep going," Tristan said, beginning to climb up the next stretch of rigging.

With a groan, Sola started to follow. He wouldn't let her climb or walk on the balloon without a harness yet, but Tristan kept Sola clambering around the rigging for a solid two hours, never allowing her to rest for more than a few seconds. By the time she was on deck again, she was out of breath and utterly exhausted.

"Same tomorrow?" asked Tristan innocently, looking, to Sola's irritation, fresh and energetic.

"Bastard."

"It was your idea!"

"And it's a good one. But you could have gone easy on me at first!"

He laughed.

"Not if you want to impress the captain in a few days time, I couldn't."

"This is about survival, not impressing Captain Sheridan," she said scathingly.

"Riiigght," drawled Gloria from behind her. "So you don't want to prove your ability in the hope you can stay aboard as crew even after this whole thing is over?"

Sola spluttered indignantly. Tristan chuckled and rested a hand on her shoulder.

"We hope she says yes too," he told her.

Henry yelling across at them ruined the moment.

"Lynch! Do some bloody work!"

Gloria glanced back at her lover, and Sola could see the deep concern in her eyes.

Staring in the mirror, Sola twisted her hair into a long braid and raised the ugly, indelicate kitchen scissors. Taking a deep breath, she hacked it off. She stared at the blonde tail in her hand, and then up at herself. The result wasn't as neat as she'd hoped – in fact, it was awful. All the same, she was relieved. All that hair just got in the way on the rigging, and on deck when it was windy. It was no wonder that Gloria always kept hers at shoulder length, and while Mac's was relatively long, it was usually braided or in a bun if she was outside. She wondered how they managed to keep theirs so neat. Certainly her first attempt at cutting her own hair was going to take some tidying up. She thought about how funny Ethan would find it, and scowled.

She checked that no one was out in the corridor before stepping into it and knocking on the door to Gloria's cabin, which was beside her own.

"Come on in," the woman called.

The room was far smaller, with a bed, and a chest of drawers, and little else beside. Gloria was lying on her bed, but on seeing who it was, swung up.

"Hey Sola... oh my god, what did you do?"

"I needed to cut it," Sola said.

"Well why didn't you *ask* you stupid girl? Get over here, sit on the floor."

She was up by the drawers, and pulled out a far daintier pair of scissors than those Sola had used. Sola did as she was told, and Gloria sat on the bed behind her.

"Stay still," the older woman warned. "You know, I was never much good at being a nanny," as she said this she began to trim, "and I think Patrick Sheridan gave up on the idea of me looking after Mac pretty quickly... but the one thing I could always do for her was this. She even had me cut it all off once, like a boy's cut, but it still looked better than what you've done to this, dear god."

"There's no need to go on about it."

"It's pretty disastrous, I just don't see why you did it."

"Convenience!"

"Convenience? Looking like an idiot is *never* convenient. If that's the aim though, I'll leave it long enough to put up. Really short hair just gets annoying; you have to cut it so often, as the captain discovered."

"Can you fix it then?" Sola said hopefully.

"Of course I can, silly girl. I just wish you'd asked me at first."

At that, Sola relaxed.

CHAPTER SEVENTEEN

Now I don't have my logbook, I must admit I miss it. I looked for James in Glasgow this morning, but as I had no idea of where he would go, the exercise was completely pointless. I did hear a rumour that bodies had been found on the dock this morning. I hope everyone on the Spitfire is unharmed.

If I want to find out for sure, I must make it to Inverness within the week. With little money and few contacts (and certainly none I would involve in this mess), I am not sure how I can achieve that.

Mac snorted and shoved the paper into her pocket. She took another sip of the terrible coffee being served in a dingy room overlooking the harbour, for dockers and sailors. Writing about her feelings was not going to help her.

Someone came into the room and her head snapped round. It was just another docker. She had found herself increasingly paranoid, seeing enemies everywhere. It made her unwilling to ask for help.

Standing, she returned the empty mug to the woman serving, and bit the bullet.

"Do you know of any ships going Inverness way?"

The woman looked out the grimy window out at the ships.

"Only the Bingley's trade ship at the far end. But they don't take passengers, love."

"Nor prisoners," Mac mumbled.

"What was that?"

"Nothing," she said, forcing a smile. "Thanks for your help."

Stowing away aboard a ship belonging to her would-be killer seemed like madness, but it might be the only way to get to Inverness in time to meet the Spitfire. And if she got way with it, it would entertain her forever. She had her jacket tied, inside out, around her waist, knowing that in an area like this, it would stand out like a sore thumb. She went a step further now and took off her waistcoat, turned it inside out, and slid it on again, leaving it hanging open and the black lining on show. Muttering a curse that she couldn't have been separated from the ship in her leather flying jacket and with her utility belt, she began to head up the docks, trying to look perfectly at ease. All the same, she got odd looks and a few catcalls – there was no way to hide her gender. She hung around at the end of the dock, wishing for the first time that she smoked. It would at least give her something to do with her hands and allow her to fit in a tiny bit more.

To pass the time, she engaged some dockers in conversation, but they weren't as friendly or informative as the ones she'd spoken to in Bristol. She couldn't really blame them - the harbour was a lot busier, they had too much to do. To her annoyance, she was still jumping at shadows, which made standing on a busy harbour a tense experience. Mac was growing impatient when, at last, the Bingley's crew opened the hold. Immediately she was hit by a sickly sweet, floral smell. Bile rose in her throat. She recognised it in an instant, and wished to god she didn't. Holding her breath, she walked closer to the ship, still keeping enough distance that the crew wouldn't ask questions. They weren't unloading the opium, but crates of Eastern fabrics. She could see the bright colours through the slats, and couldn't help smiling to herself. It was an import she approved of, and she was sure Tamsin would have some in her shop before long. It might be worth another trip to Bristol. She sobered in an instant. If she ever got back to her bloody ship, it might. They loaded the crates on to trolleys, which they began to wheel away. Now was her moment. Her heart stopped for a second in anticipation, and then she started walking. She wanted to look casual, but couldn't help rushing. Stepping onto the ramp, she glanced around, and then, throwing caution to the wind, ran inside the vessel. The stench inside was overwhelming, and it was all she could do not to vomit. She forced herself further inside; towards the boxes that held the vile drug. Crouching down, she crawled between two large crates and curled into a ball behind one of them. And she waited, hoping desperately that they weren't planning on unloading the opium too. Thankfully, after a while she heard the cargo hatch slam closed, and she was plunged into darkness. Mac didn't know how long she sat there, but she did know her body was aching from the discomfort of the position by the time the ship began to move. Within ten minutes, she had another issue. The swaying of the ship - so different from the motion of an airship - combined with the nauseating stench from the opium was making her feel sick. She snorted to herself, imaging what the crew would say when (she made sure she thought 'when') she told them that she'd gotten seasick. Incapable of staying still any longer, she crawled out of the hole she'd made for herself and stretched her muscles. Her eyes had adjusted a little to the darkness, but there wasn't much to see: just crates on crates of foul-smelling opium. The hold was large though, so she wandered around it, taking her time, and trying to tread softly.

After what felt like several hours (and she certainly hoped it was no shorter than that), the boredom was just about killing Mac. Having had so much to do recently, she'd have thought some forced relaxation would be good for her, but she would have preferred to have a book, and some light to read it by. And, for that matter, not to be stowing away aboard the ship of a man who apparently wanted her dead. Still unable to piece together the puzzle in her head - what connected her parents with George and Beatrice Austin, with Duke Russell Bernard, with Edward Bingley... giving up, she crawled back into the space she had made, twisting herself into an uncomfortable position so she could lie on the floor. Given that she hadn't been able to sleep on her own ship, she doubted it would be possible on someone else's, but there was little else to do. She may as well try.

CHAPTER EIGHTEEN

If I thought that my body hurt after that first shift in the crow's nest, it is nothing compared to after Tristan's 'training'. He is relentless. Yes, it was my idea. Yes, I asked him to. But oh my god, he has taken it up with gusto. Rob and Gloria just laugh, and Ethan worries, but he has been very good at keeping it to himself. He understands, I think, how important it is to me that I am good at this. My being busy also gives him more time to work on his inventions, something I think slowed when we were spending almost every waking minute together. I still try to make time to see him though - the workshop is a good place to hide from Tristan when I desperately need a break. He knows where I am, but seems terrified to go into it. Something about an explosion that happened once? It sounds like a story I'd like to hear, but Ethan is too embarrassed to tell it to me.

On the positive side, a few days of intense training later, I am almost used to the pain. Maybe this is how the crew survives: they are not impervious, just accustomed. In honesty, I am more concerned about the absence of Captain Sheridan and James. I didn't realise how fragile the community aboard the Spitfire is, how easily disturbed. Henry has become very serious and even quieter. Gloria seems to hover between worry and anger. Mostly anger, however, he is incensing her.

As predicted, we have just arrived in Inverness, exactly at midday. Tristan has decided that with no cargo to unload, and no more ship-flying duties to undertake, this is the perfect time to test my progress. So now, with terror in my heart, I must head back up to the deck again.

Tristan had her follow him around the rigging for half an hour, moving slower than he usually would, but faster than she ever had before. Then, for the first time since that shift in the crow's nest, he took her up onto the balloon. She crawled on, as she had done before, and rested at the top on her hands and knees. Tristan crouched comfortably in front of her.

"Lift your hands," he said, waving his in front of her face for emphasis.

Biting back a sarcastic comment, she did so, and slowly straightened her back so she was kneeling on the metal.

"Now up onto your feet, like me."

The previous couple of days training with Tristan had taught Sola that the worst thing to say was "I can't," as he seemed to take it as a personal challenge. She rested her hands back down at her sides, and used them to steady herself as she rolled back onto the balls of her feet. When she had her balance, she lifted them again.

He grinned, and turned from her, heading toward the crow's nest. Keeping as low as possible, even though she felt like an idiot, Sola did the same, carefully avoiding looking at the city far below her. On reaching the crow's nest, she grabbed it and climbed in as quickly as she could, glad for the security of the basket around her.

"Brilliant," congratulated Tristan, leaning on the outside edge of the nest. "Now we've just got to get down, and we'll do some shooting."

Sola forced herself not to complain. Climbing down was infinitely worse than climbing up, as you couldn't see where you were going, or your next foothold. She wasn't doing it quickly at all, which Tristan delighted in reminding her of. Gritting her teeth, she said nothing and stretched her leg down.

Ethan had constructed a thick plywood target for them to practice with. It was now riddled with bullet holes, several of them quite far from the centre, and many not in the painted ring of circles at all. Recently though, her aim had been improving. She still pulled to the left, which had been Mac's constant complaint. Tristan held out his gun to her, and she reached to take it. She wrapped her hand around the grip, but he didn't let go, and frowned at the gun in confusion.

"What is it?"

"Are you left handed?" he asked.

She looked down, realising she had subconsciously reached out with her left hand.

"Yes," she said, almost having forgotten herself. "I was encouraged at school to pretend otherwise. I guess I really am losing all my good manners here."

"No wonder you're not shooting straight," he said, as though solving a great mystery. "These guns are made with right-hand grips, and you've been trying to hold them as though you're right handed too. Reverse your grip, for a start, and I'll speak with Ethan about guns."

"He can make a left handed gun?"

"Patrick Sheridan made one from scratch, as I recall. Neat little pistol that worked like a dream, except I never met a right-hander who could shoot it straight. But we'll just have Ethan alter the grip on one for now, leave the bigger challenge for later."

"Sheridan was left handed?" she asked, somehow liking that she shared this with the previous captain.

"He was. He said to me that he had been taught to repress it, but if he wanted to invent, he had to use his hands as delicately and precisely as possible, and that meant embracing which was dominant, even if society had what he called an 'absurd stigma' against it."

Sola smiled at the thought. She switched the gun into her left hand, doing her best to create the mirror image of what she'd been trying for so far. Taking careful aim, she fired. The balcony splintered. Tristan burst into hysterical laughter.

"Don't laugh! I thought this was going to fix it!" she said, feeling for the first time since about the age of two a desperate desire to stamp her foot.

"It'll take some getting used to, I expect. You were getting proficient with the right. Keep trying, we can mend the ship."

"The captain's going to love you for saying that," she muttered, but taking his advice, aimed again.

This time she hit the plywood at least, though not the painted target. But as she kept firing, the progression was far quicker than it had been with her right hand. By the end of a round of ammunition, she was within the inner rings with almost every shot.

"That's incredible!" she said, laughing. "Just that from changing which hand I use."

"Wait until you're using the right grip too," said Tristan, grinning. "That'll do us for this afternoon I think. I'm going to go and get a decent meal in the city, if the laugh-fest that is Henry Large will allow it. You go distract Ethan. Take that gun with you, tell him about the grip thing, would you?"

"Don't you need it?" she asked, not daring to hope that she was actually being given a weapon.

"I have another couple," he said. "Keep it. You deserve it. You've worked bloody hard, and I promise you the captain is going to respect you for it."

She couldn't wipe the smile from her face. Resisting the temptation to skip down the workshop – she couldn't imagine Gloria or Captain Sheridan skipping – she instead walked at a brisk pace, looking forward to seeing Ethan. She grabbed for the door handle, before remembering herself and knocking. Now that she no longer felt obliged to out of courtesy, it was hard to remember there was a safety consideration as well.

"Come in."

Ethan turned around as she stepped into the room, and smiled broadly on seeing her.

"Looks like someone had a good morning," he teased. "You signed a contract yet?"

"I was up on the balloon," she boasted, grinning, although feeling slightly guilty for the green tinge his face took on at the thought. "And Tristan worked out what's been going wrong with my shooting – I'm left handed. I didn't even *think* about it. So he wants you to re-mould the grip on this gun so I can use it," she finished, sliding the weapon in front of him.

"Left handed?" he said, with a smile. "That's easily done, I can have it for you by tomorrow?"

She eyed him critically, a thought occurring to her.

"Are you a good marksman?" she asked. "I've never really seen you shoot."

"I'm an excellent marksman," Ethan replied dryly.

"I'm serious."

He looked offended.

"So am I!"

"Prove it."

Laughing, he stood and began to walk towards the door. When she didn't follow, he turned back and glanced at her.

"Well hurry up, Sola. I can hardly shoot in here."

Grinning, she leapt up after him.

Out on the deck, the plywood target was still in the open. Ethan drew the pistol from his belt, a more refined weapon than the one Sola had been using, elegantly made. Standing at twice the distance Sola usually would, he took his stance almost casually, and fired off three rounds.

To Sola's surprise, three holes had wiped out the circumference of the bull's-eye.

"Woah, you weren't joking," she said, awed.

He lowered his mouth to her ear.

"Steadiness and precision suit me," he whispered.

A pleasant thrill ran through her body. Not thinking about it, she placed a hand on the back of his neck and tugged his face to hers, kissing him firmly. It was a wolf-whistle from the other side of the deck that reminded her they weren't in the privacy of his workshop or her room. She pulled away and twisted her head to see Gloria and Rob laughing hysterically. Casually, with an ease and familiarity that would have shocked her before, she stuck her middle finger up at them and pulled Ethan down for another kiss.

CHAPTER NINETEEN

Bored bored bored. Very little to do here. Very dark. Too dark to write, even if I did have my log with me. Have resorted to narrating thoughts in my head. Other people might call it talking to myself. Going crazy. Oddly, also feel saner than I have done in quite a while. Haven't had time to think like this since Father was killed and all this Sola Austin nonsense started.

That morning, or what Mac chose to call morning, she had woken slowly. For the few minutes before she remembered the situation, she was utterly relaxed. It was the best she had slept since her father died. Almost certainly there would be a number of psychological explanations for this – maybe it was that she had no memories of him in this place, or maybe she had just reached the level of stress, exhaustion and frustration that would cause her brain to give up and shut down.

After crawling out of her makeshift bed, she walked a few times around the hold, stretching out all her muscles again. It was then that the possibility of physical wastage occurred to her. With no food and no light, and no exercise, she could decline quickly. Immediately she regretted thinking of food. Pulling off her waistcoat and untying her jacket, which was still around her waist, she dropped to the ground and began press-ups. Fifty later, she rolled over and started on sit-ups. She'd followed a strict exercise regime ever since she was old enough to do so without hurting herself. Here, the apparatus was more limited– there was no rigging to race up and down, no beams to use for pull ups, but she did her best to adapt. One crate became a stand for her to place her hands on while she lowered and lifted her body, and another she used to step onto and off of as quickly as she could. She kept going until sweat had drenched her clothes and was dripping off her forehead, then collapsed onto the ground and sat, breathing heavily. Maybe it hadn't been the best of ideas. She had no water, and had just sweated out plenty of her body's reserves. On the other hand, her head was wonderfully clear. Her mood had been inexplicably lifted by the activity. For some reason, despite the awfulness of the situation, she was grinning widely. She used the discarded waistcoat to wipe her face of sweat, then entwined it with her jacket and tied the twisted material around her waist again. Having exerted herself enough physically, she turned to thinking.

For once, she bypassed the many mysteries currently in her life, accepting for a brief time that she was incapable of solving them. Instead she thought of the Spitfire.

Bodies on the pier suggested they had been attacked. She didn't know if any of the bodies were of her crew, but clung to the hope that that detail would surely have been included in the rumours. The crews of the surrounding airships at the dock would have recognized them. That didn't account for whether any of them had been injured, however.

Truly confusing was how any attackers had gotten inside the ship. She had instructed Henry to lock all but the back balcony door. If they'd gone in through the back balcony, they would have found themselves stuck in her study, as she'd made sure the other door there was locked, with no key in the room. Again, she had thought of this eventuality, and told Henry if it happened to make sure Sola slept in the workshop, so she would be nowhere near them, and otherwise to leave them there until they gave up or battered the door down. There was a clearer explanation, however. A startlingly clear one, which fitted with all of the facts and made perfect sense, and the only reason she had ignored it or forced it out of her thoughts so far was that she just couldn't stand it being the truth. Mac sunk her head into her hands, her good mood ruined.

Her hunger and thirst increased. The hunger nagged gently, an aching pain in her stomach; just enough to remind her of how long it had been since she ate. The thirst, on the other hand, prodded and pinched and stung, refusing to be ignored or put aside. Her head hurt and her throat hurt and her mouth was dry and any attempt she made to distract herself from the truth of it was doomed to fail.

Eventually, she cracked. Walking slowly to the staircase at the far end of the hold, she climbed it, hitting her head on the hatch when she reached the top.

"Ouch."

She rubbed it gently, then reached up a hand and pressed against the ceiling above her. To her infinite relief, it caved, letting in a little more light as it opened. She pulled herself up into the corridor, silently giving thanks for its emptiness. A glance out of a porthole gave the approximate time, as she could see a sliver of the disappearing sun.

There was a pattering of feet. Her heart stopped for an instant and then began to beat irregularly, like a malfunctioning engine in her chest. She turned around slowly, knowing there was no chance of getting back into the hold. When she saw it, she laughed. Padding down the corridor was a large brown dog. She knew dogs could be violent, but one look in the face of this one, as it walked toward her, wagging its tail so hard that its whole body wiggled, convinced her that it was perfectly safe.

"Hello," she said, grinning.

It wagged its tail harder still, eventually reaching her and shoving its head toward her. She obliged it, scratching around the neck in a way that seemed to please the animal.

"Aren't you just lovely," she said, still chuckling gently. "I wonder what your name is?"

Obviously, the dog did not answer.

"You are beautiful," she said, ignoring the salty, grimy smell from its fur.

To her relief, it seemed well fed and perfectly content – so often the opposite was true of animals aboard ships.

"Do you know where I can find some food?" she asked.

She was mostly thinking aloud, but the dog's eyes seemed to light up, and it turned from her and began to walk. Figuring that she hadn't a better plan, she followed. He led her to a door at the end of the corridor and began to scratch at it. She could see several marks on the wood from it doing the same thing in the past. Heart in throat, she knocked. When there was no answer, she turned the handle and stepped inside. The first thing she set eyes on was the water barrel. Not bothering with finding a cup, she cupped it into her hands and scooped it messily into her mouth, desperately quenching her thirst. When she felt well watered, she moved on to examining the cupboards. Scared of taking too much, she found a few biscuits, and ate them hurriedly. Glancing at the large, shining eyes of her canine companion, she couldn't stop herself from giving the dog one as well. She jammed a few more into her pockets, and then went back to looking through the cupboards, finding an empty water-skin in the back of one of them. Hoping that it wouldn't be missed, she filled the container from the barrel. The dog was reluctant to leave the galley, but she forced it to. Tempted as she was to try and find a way outdoors, to breathe fresh air again, she knew it was far too dangerous to contemplate. Mac felt a little guilty as she slipped back down into the hold, with the dog staring at her with sad, reproachful eyes. She didn't know whether it was for the loss of her company or that she was taking the biscuits in her pocket with her.

"I'll come back up," she promised, not knowing whether it was true or not. "Thanks for your help."

And she plunged herself back into darkness.

The biscuits and water she had stolen sustained Mac for a further two days. She kept up the exercise, though not as intensively. Once she had taken the last sip of water, she decided it was time to go up again.

In honesty, she knew it was stupid. She could go a little further on the water she had just drank, after all. But there was a part of her that wanted to see the dog again, that missed its affectionate companionship, even if the affection was driven by a desire for food. The animal appeared shortly after she climbed into the corridor: it must have been in some way conditioned to the opening of the hold.

On seeing her, it grinned in that strange animalistic way, and immediately began badgering her for attention. When she'd stroked it a little, it rolled over, wanting a belly rub. Mac obliged.

"A girl, huh? What a gorgeous girl. They don't mind female dogs on nautical ships then? Nice to know the prejudice doesn't span every species."

The dog sighed in pleasure and flopped over. Mac laughed.

"What I'd give for your life right now, honey," she said sadly. "Now I need water. Coming with?"

The animal was on her feet immediately. Despite the tension that said someone could appear at any moment, it was difficult for Mac to be anything but happy in such good company. She wasn't sure if dogs took well to heights, but the thought of having one aboard the Spitfire was brilliant. She opened the galley door, and stared in shock at the two men inside.

I didn't knock. Mac internally let loose a string of venomous self-criticism.

"Who the fuck are you, and why the fuck are you on board my ship?"

CHAPTER TWENTY

This evening we will leave Inverness if Captain Sheridan does not appear. I just trusted that she would make it, as did the rest of the crew, I believe. And yet here we are, faced with the prospect of leaving her, possibly forever. The mood is grim on the Spitfire today. Even Tristan is tense; even Rob is miserable; and even Ethan and I are not enough to comfort each other. I find myself preferring privacy at the moment, and thankfully he seems to agree.

Sola sighed and set down the journal. There were no words to truly describe her mood. She chose to go to the back balcony, knowing that no one else would stray there, even in Mac's absence. The city of Inverness was spread out below her, but the network of streets held none of its usual fascination. She had been into the city, but couldn't drag up appropriate interest in it.

Feeling mildly guilty, she turned to the door into Mac's study. They hadn't bothered to lock it, which seemed idiotic now. Telling herself she was just going to look for a key, she went inside. Despite her good intentions, she was immediately drawn to the large red book on the desk, which she knew was Captain Sheridan's log.

She flicked through the entries, eyes resting on the passage:

"Austin and Ethan's relationship continues, though the most I see of it is loving looks across the crew lounge. I have no idea whether they've taken it to her bedroom yet, and no desire to think about it (damn Riddle for putting the thought in my head last night). Disturbing, as that is the bed where Marcus and I... anyway."

Sola spluttered in shock. She'd known from the photo that Marcus Tate and Mac Sheridan had some sort of friendship but... and no wonder the captain had found the gossip of Sola running off with a Negro so amusing! Not to mention it being the same bed. *Thanks, Captain. Really didn't need to know that.*

She knew she should walk away, but couldn't help flicking back. The next she bothered to take time over read:

"I was thrown by the idea that Father planned to hand over the captaincy to me. Did he really think I was capable of this? I'm barely managing. Though I suppose he thought he would be around to advise me. I wish he were, and not just because I miss him. I could certainly do with an advisor. Anyway, there is no point in dwelling on my inadequacies. This is my job, and I have to do it, and that's all there is to it.

No matter how many times I see it, the sight of opium-riddled beggars repels me. I hope it haunts Lady Austin also – the aristocracy must take no small part of the blame for this disease of society."

It had obviously been after their visit to Tamsin Worthing's shop in Bristol. There were a number of interesting elements in it. She would have wondered about blaming the aristocracy for opium addiction before the crew had told her about Edward Bingley. There was no doubt he had close ties with a lot of aristocrats and government officials, so she accepted her social class was linked to the issue, though she objected to the thought of having any personal hand in it.

More intriguing was "I'm barely managing" and "my inadequacies". Sheridan had never expressed or even accidentally displayed anything resembling self-doubt as far as she remembered. For the first time, Sola considered how hard it would be for a girl barely older than herself to run an airship, not to mention grieve her father at the same time, with the added stress of kidnapping someone to honour his last request. She was suddenly overwhelmed by pity. Images from the last couple of weeks flashed through her head. The captain excusing herself from card games when the night was still young, deep black circles under her eyes. And she had assumed it was because of her. Sola was embarrassed. She closed the logbook, telling herself that Captain Sheridan would read her journal if the opportunity presented itself.

There was something wrong about the image of Henry in this study, writing up an entry in the log, or keeping the books. As much as she had originally disliked Sheridan, an airship run by Henry Large would be a totally different place, and she wasn't sure she would like it. She looked out the porthole by Mac's desk, and grimaced at the sight of a sun that was entering the second half of the day.

Come on, Captain.

She wandered across to the bookshop, pulling out a well-worn paperback, a copy of *Alice's Adventures in Wonderland*. For some reason, she couldn't see Mackenzie Sheridan curling up with Carroll's story. She opened it to see a handwritten dedication on the title page.

Dearest Aislin,

Happy birthday, my darling friend. I can't help thinking you could stand a little more nonsense in that practical life of yours!

Hoping to see you and Patrick very soon.

Yours with great affection,

Bea

She stared at the words in shock, not because of what they said – it was hardly the first piece of evidence that the two women had been friends – but because she realised she had never seen her mother's handwriting before. In the first chapter, there was quote underlined in black ink that had soaked into the paper: "So many out-of-the-way things had happened lately, that Alice had begun to think that very few things indeed were really impossible."

Sola smiled, feeling as though the sentiment suited her own recent life changes perfectly. She wondered if it was her mother or Aislin Mackenzie who had picked it out. All of a sudden, the thought that she would never meet her mother or her namesake hit her, and she sighed, slipping the book back onto the shelf.

She let herself back out onto the balcony (they still hadn't found the key to unlock the main door) and headed up onto the deck again.

That evening, when the sun was beginning its final descent, the whole of the remaining crew was on deck. They watched over the city urgently, hoping for a miracle.

"Very few things are really impossible," Sola whispered, so only Ethan could hear her.

"What do you mean?" he asked.

She just shook her head. Her heart lurched as the ship began to move. She looked up to the deck, where Henry was steering them ever so slowly away from the deck. Part of her desperately wanted to stop him, but she knew it had to be done at some point.

Then Tristan yelled.

"Wait!"

They all whirled around, to see a familiar figure running up the dock. The ship kept moving.

"Henry!" she shouted.

"Stop the ship, it's her!" yelled Rob, his accent more pronounced than she'd ever heard it. But for some reason the Spitfire continued to drift away from the dock.

Tristan grabbed something from a cupboard and threw something over the side of the deck, while Rob was running up to stop Henry.

Tristan had thrown a rope ladder, and was holding it tightly. Sola couldn't turn away, watching the captain sprint along the dock and, to her shock, leap off the end. She stopped breathing. The seconds seemed to drag out as Mac flew through the air, then she grabbed the ladder and crashed into the side of the ship. Tristan began to pull, and Ethan was at his side in an instant. The two men pulled up the ladder at impressive speeds, and when Mac was level with the railing, they grabbed her under the arms and tugged her upwards, all three of them collapsing into a heap on the deck.

They gradually sorted themselves out, one by one climbing back to their feet. Sola got her first good look at the captain. The other woman was blatantly exhausted; there was a pallor to her skin, bags under her eyes, and a sheen of sweat over her face. Her clothes were dirty and ragged. Her hair was in a tangled mess.

"What happened to you?" Sola asked.

"I really don't have time to tell you right now," Mac replied, sounding as bad as she looked.

"Why not?" asked Tristan.

Mac took a deep breath and blinked a few times.
"Because I'm about to faint."
Just as she finished saying it, she did.

CHAPTER TWENTY-ONE

Being on the Spitfire feels incredible. I have missed her and my crew so much. I feel horrible that we had to leave James in Glasgow, and hope that is not the last we will see of him. That said, there were some crewmembers I didn't want to see today. It hurts my heart to think of it.

Mac woke on a sofa in the lounge, to see Austin and Ethan quietly playing cards at a table opposite. She slowly stretched out, feeling tender and already seeing the hints of bruises forming from where she had slammed into the side of the ship, never mind the pain in her legs from riding so far and running so fast. When she had been discovered (or rather foolishly revealed herself) on the Bingley's ship, she turned and ran, knowing there was no good explanation. She sprinted up several flights of stairs, eventually hitting the deck, and threw herself off the side of the ship. It was pure good fortune that they were sticking close to the coastline on their journey. It was the better part of an hour before she managed to swim to shore. Her plan had been to find the nearest town and beg for assistance. Then she had seen the horses. They were just grazing in a field. She knew it was wrong, but it was easy to justify it to herself when she reasoned that she had less than two days to reach Inverness, and a road marker indicated there were seventy more miles to go.

Her sodden jacket didn't make the best of saddles, but it was better than nothing, and so she set off, galloping on a stolen horse towards her ship. She left the animal, worn out, at the bottom of the docks in Inverness, and hoped that someone would find it and take care of it, but she had more pressing worries at the time. Watching the Spitfire begin to pull away was horrific, inspiring the temporary madness that drove her to leap off a dock at least a hundred feet high.

She supposed she should let them know that she was awake, so she pulled herself up into a sitting position.

"You're awake!" exclaimed Austin.

"Thank you for pointing that out, Lady Austin," she said, with no real venom.

Ethan poured her a glass of water and passed it over.

"Thanks," she said, tipping the glass to her lips and soon finishing it. To think she had taken water for granted! The taste was wonderful. "Is Henry on board?"

"Why wouldn't he be?" said Ethan, frowning.

To her surprise, Mac saw a glimmer of understanding in Austin's eyes.

"I'd rather deal with that in front of everyone," she said apologetically to Ethan. "I don't want to go through it more than once, to be honest."

At the end of that sentence she glanced at Austin, who seemed on the brink of asking what had happened. The other girl smiled and nodded slightly.

"And first I need a bath," she said, laughing a little. "Can you two arrange for everyone to be back here in an hour's time?"

The couple nodded in tandem. Slowly, due to the stiffness that had invaded her whole body, Mac left the room. She felt in her pocket, relieved to find the iron key to her study, and grabbed the most comfortable clothes she could find before heading into the bathroom next door. The hot water was a wonderful relief. She lay there for a while before she even thought to wash herself and make an effort towards unknotting her hair.

Once she felt human again, and looked vaguely presentable, she walked back through to the lounge. As promised, the whole crew was gathered there. She spread her hands in a questioning gesture.

"Tell me what happened," she said.

They were silent for a little while.

"I was on deck," Austin began. "Up in the rigging, practicing. I saw the men climb aboard. There were four of them. I didn't know how to stop them, so I just let them go in..."

She broke eye contact, looking at the floor in shame.

"I should bloody hope so," Mac said. "Getting you killed is exactly what we're trying to avoid. They all died?"

Gloria nodded and took over.

"I think they went to Sola's cabin first, but when no one was there, three of them came here, and one went down to Ethan's workshop. Tristan, Rob and I were in here, we shot two pretty quickly but the third took cover and so did we. Henry had been in his cabin, he came through when he heard the shooting and killed the last one."

"And the one who went to you, Ethan?"

Ethan coughed.

"Sola followed shortly after him. Before I'd even thought about grabbing a gun, she shot him in the back."

Mac looked up at the girl in surprise.

"How're you coping?" she asked.

Sola managed a halfhearted smile.

"Not so bad. I don't regret it, if that's what you're asking."

"It is and it isn't," Mac said. "So they knew the way around the ship, obviously."

Rob frowned.

"Now you mention it, Captain..."

"And the door wasn't locked," she continued, acknowledging Rob with a nod. She looked over at Henry.

"Slipped my mind, Captain," he said. "Can't apologise enough."

She closed her eyes and breathed in deeply before opening them again. The momentary flicker of panic and guilt on his face was enough to confirm everything she wished she was wrong about.

"Henry."

"I promise it won't happen again."

"Don't take me for a fool, Mr Large," Mac said harshly, forcing a cold tone. "What did they give you? Was it just for money? Don't I pay you enough?"

"I don't know what you're talking about, Mac."

"*Don't* call me Mac right now, you traitorous bastard."

The Spitfire Project

Everyone else in the room was staring at him in shock. Mac wondered if they believed her or if they couldn't. Two weeks beforehand, she wouldn't have been able to.

"I guess you panicked when you saw me running towards the dock," she said. "I can't imagine what you thought you'd achieve by trying to leave me."

"I didn't..." Henry began, but his voice trailed into silence. "You've got to understand..."

"I'd love to understand, Henry, but I don't. I know my father saw you as a friend. That you would do this to his daughter and the girl he gave his life to protect... I would *love* to understand. Please, if there is an explanation, give it."

The man fell silent, but Gloria spoke up.

"I think I can explain, Captain."

Mac flicked her eyes to the woman in horror.

"Gloria, don't tell me you –"

"No! God, Mackenzie, no, of course not. I would never."

Running her hand through her hair, Mac nodded.

"Sorry," she said. "Go on."

Gloria paused and swallowed, her face setting into an expression of grim determination.

"I'm pregnant," she said.

Mac could feel her jaw dropping, and forced herself to close it. Tristan didn't have any such control; his was practically on the floor.

"I don't know if congratulations is the right sentiment in the circumstances," Mac said, "but congratulations all the same. Yours, Henry, I assume?"

Henry nodded, looking every inch a beaten man.

"I fail to see how it explains Henry's actions," she said, turning back to Gloria.

"He doesn't have any money," Gloria said, an icy edge to her voice.

Mac glanced around the room.

"I *am* paying you enough, aren't I?"

"It's not that," Gloria said quickly. "It's that he gambles."

"We all gamble," said Mac. "James lost his money to Austin, of all people."

The mention of James did nothing for the atmosphere of the room.

"He can't stop," Gloria added. "He lost everything."

She stared at Henry, who was resting his head in his hands.

"Oh you stupid, stupid bastard," she whispered. "Why didn't you come to me? I wouldn't have... I'd have... my god, Henry."

Henry, who was large in not just name, but also stature, had never looked smaller to her.

"I'm going to drop you off in the next town we reach," she said, giving up. "I'm assuming you have the money they gave you. Use it how you please, transport yourself to a city and get a job, gamble it all away if you wish."

"What about Gloria?" Henry said hoarsely. His head twitched as if to look around at the woman, but he didn't.

"It's Gloria's decision whether she wants anything more to do with you. I assure you, she and the child will be looked after." Mac stood, barely having the energy for it. She walked over to Rob and passed him a key. "Please ensure Henry is locked in his cabin tonight, he is no longer free to do as he pleases aboard this ship. Henry, I suggest you pack. Gloria... you and I must speak, but I would prefer to wait until tomorrow."

"Of course, Captain."

"Good night, everyone," she said, feeling the lie in the sentence. There had been very little good about it for any of them.

CHAPTER TWENTY-TWO

I don't want to believe it. Yet it makes such sickeningly perfect sense. The way he has been acting recently, especially since we left Glasgow, has just been too strange. And he didn't deny it in the end. We seem to be hemorrhaging crew at the moment. It was difficult flying from Glasgow to Inverness, missing two of our number, and now it seems we will be missing two again. I hope James shows up somewhere, somehow. We really do need him, and not just for the manpower.

I thought about going to bed, but I'm not sure I'll be able to sleep tonight. Captain Sheridan went to her study over an hour ago, and maybe she is sleeping, but I somehow doubt it.

Sola looked at the sentence she had just written. Hadn't she resolved to make more of an effort with the captain? She was hardly going to rest, and Ethan had gone to soak up his distress in gears and who-knew-what-else. Setting her mind on the idea, she stepped into the corridor and looked at the opposite door. What if the captain *was* sleeping? She was clearly exhausted, after all... Sola decided to just peek inside. She opened the door and peered in, to see Captain Sheridan sitting at the round table, sipping a glass of whiskey.

"It's not healthy to drink alone, you know," she said, opening the door fully and stepping inside the room.

"Lady Austin. I thought you were raised with manners, were you never taught to knock?"

The captain stood, and for a second Sola thought she was about to be thrown out. Instead Mac turned and walked under the mezzanine, to the chest of drawers. She pulled a tumbler and a decanter full of whiskey from the top drawer, and poured another glass. Returning to the table, she placed it in front of the other seat, and returned to her own.

"Now I'm not alone," she said.

Surprised by the invitation, Sola closed the door and sat down before the captain could change her mind.

"Is something bothering you, Lady Austin?"

Sola shrugged.

"Just didn't think I'd be able to sleep."

"Are you having nightmares?"

The question was immediate, the tone familiar. With a burst of insight, Sola realised nightmares must be something Captain Sheridan had suffered from, and maybe still did.

"One or two."

Mac nodded, and sipped some of the amber liquid from her glass.

"Sorry you had to go through that."

"It's hardly your fault."

"It is."

Sola looked quizzically at her.

"I'm meant to be protecting you. So when I trust your safety to someone, and they put you in danger..." she shook her head, drinking again. "It is my fault."

"You can't be expected to be omniscient."

"Thank you."

Raising her glass to her lips, Sola thanked god that she had drank whiskey with Jesse before, and was prepared for the way it would burn her throat. The sensation wasn't entirely unpleasant when you knew it was coming, but it had been horrible the first time.

"What happened to you, then, to get you in such a state?"

Mac laughed.

"You're pretty blunt, Lady Austin," she said. "It's not a trait I would have expected you to have."

"I'm curious," Sola replied with a smile.

"I was poisoned at the trade conference," the captain said. "I woke up on a ship captained by a friend of mine, who had saved my life. She told me about the Spitfire leaving, so I knew something must have happened to you as well."

"Poisoned? Who by?"

"Most likely suspect is Edward Bingley," said Mac, letting out a disbelieving laugh. "It happened after drinking champagne he gave me."

"Why would Edward Bingley poison you?"

"I honestly have no idea."

"But your friend didn't give you a lift to Inverness?"

"She offered." Mac snorted. "I wish I'd taken her up on it after the journey I had, but I didn't want her to get involved. If a Duke and the overlord of the shipping industry are both tied into this somehow, it's serious stuff."

"So how did you get here?"

"I stowed away on a trade ship. Not an airship, either, the nautical kind. A Bingley's ship, actually – you've got to love the irony in that. It worked out fine for a few days, but then I made a stupid mistake and got myself caught."

Sola's eyes widened. Stowaways were heavily frowned on in *all* types of shipping, and she didn't like to think of what could have happened.

"You got away?"

"Took a flying leap and swam to shore. Not as easy as one might think."

"Were you near the city then?"

"Not too far. I stole a horse from a field and rode almost solidly for the next few days. Poor animal is buggered, I hope someone good finds it."

"Your body must hurt all over."

Mac chuckled.

"In places I didn't even know existed," she admitted. "Tristan mentioned you two have been doing a little training, so I imagine you're not exactly rested either." She raised a glass to Sola. "You and I will take a day off tomorrow, deal?"

Sola clinked her glass against it.

"Deal."

The two women drank together.

CHAPTER TWENTY-THREE

Leaving Henry was a wrench, despite what he has done. I am equal parts sympathetic and furious, but most of all I am hurt. I cannot fathom one of our own doing this to us. Did he not realise he would also be placing Gloria and the child in danger?

That, of course, is another situation I must soon deal with. I meant it when I said to Lady Austin that I'd be taking a physical break today, but the mental stresses of captaincy are relentless.

I also must accept that long-term planning is required here. The Spitfire is plainly in great danger, and living day-to-day might not do the trick for much longer. I admit, I have begun to think of abroad, for a while at least, though it feels like running away. Perhaps with such mysterious and formidable enemies, a little running is in order.

She found Gloria in her cabin, after looking on deck and in the crew lounge. In hindsight, it made sense that the woman would not be in public after the emotional mess of saying goodbye to the traitorous father of her child.

"Shall we go to the study?" she said, only because Gloria's cabin had no place to sit.

Once they were resting there, Mac opened the conversation.

"I have no problem with a baby on board an airship, you know that. I was born on this ship. But I am concerned that it's not the safest place for you if anything goes wrong in the pregnancy."

"I hadn't even thought about that," said Gloria. "There's so much to think about, and I've barely even..."

The Spitfire Project

"It's been a stressful time," Mac soothed. "Let's just make sure the child is your number one priority right now. Assuming you want it, of course?"

Gloria nodded fervently.

"I mean, I thought about it," she admitted. "Especially after last night and that whole thing with Henry. But I do want it. I've always wanted a family, and I'm not getting any younger."

Mac smiled a little. Gloria was in her mid-thirties, which was a little old for a woman to have children, but by no means unheard of or impossible.

"Then I think the best thing to do is give you a few months of paid leave. Is there someone you can stay with?"

"My brother," she responded immediately. "He'll be fine about it."

"Where does he live?"

"Birmingham."

"We'll fly towards Birmingham now then," Mac said. "We're just drifting as it is, it'll do good to have a goal. How far along are you?"

"Roughly three months."

Mac stared in shock at Gloria's stomach, which was still flat.

"Bloody hell."

"It was pretty easy to tell myself that I'd explain everything to you once I started to show," laughed Gloria.

"We'll head to Birmingham and drop you at your brother's," Mac continued, shaking her head in disbelief. "Stay there, relax, and when you've had the baby, let me know what you want to do. Your child is welcome aboard the Spitfire, but it's a decision only you can make."

"Can you cope with losing crew like this?" Gloria asked, frowning.

She had quickly honed in on Mac's biggest problem.

"I haven't given up on James Riddle just yet," Mac smiled, though the expression was more than slightly forced.

"Mac, if you need me... I don't need to go just yet."

"I think it works best," Mac reassured her, not mentioning her ideas of going abroad for a while. "Though I do hope you'll choose to return."

Gloria stood and stretched out a hand. Grinning, Mac followed her lead, and reached out to shake it.

"You're doing great, Mackenzie," Gloria said softly.

"That's the second time you've called me that in two days, you know."

"Reminds me of when you were little. There was a debate in the crew over whether to shorten your name to 'Mac' or 'Kenzie' – I kept neutral by always using the full thing."

"It's hard to think you've known me for so long."

Gloria squeezed her hand.

"Like I said, you're doing great."

"Thank you. You're going to be an amazing mother."

She laughed.

"I hope so, Mac. I really do."

Watching Gloria walk out the door hurt, even though logically Mac knew it was a while before they'd have to say the real goodbye.

It was easy to forget her problems, however, as they drifted down the coast of Scotland. Mac spent as much time as possible on deck, enjoying the light and fresh air after those days in the opium-scented hold. Seeing a storm building on the horizon, she reluctantly turned the ship inland. The salty smell of the sea was soon lost to greenery and a network of rivers. She chose one of the larger waterways to follow and continued down it, flying relatively low in case the storm came earlier than she was anticipating. There was a road running along the river, and she looked down, wondering with a smile whether it was one of the ones she'd ridden along in the previous days. That was when she saw a group of people standing by the roadside at a cart, waving their arms desperately in the air. It said something about how Mac had changed that her first reaction was suspicion: was it a trap of some kind? Soon though, logic took over. There was no way that anyone would be able to predict they'd be in this spot at this time. Concerned, she lowered the ship further, hovering above them.

Lady Austin, Tristan, and Gloria were already on deck, and Ethan and Rob soon appeared to see why they had stopped, as Mac hung over the balcony.

"What's happened?"

"A cart went into the water!" one man yelled back.

Now they were closer, she could see the tracks on the riverbank, and that a couple of the group were soaked through.

"Is everyone out?" she called.

"No!" screamed a woman who was drenched. "My husband!"

"Fuck," Mac muttered.

She shoved her jacket off her shoulders onto the deck, and started unbuckling her belt.

"Can you swim?" she said, turning to Sola, knowing the answer from the rest of her crew.

"What?" Sola replied, in utter confusion.

"Never mind," she snapped, exasperated.

She climbed over the balcony, took a deep breath, and dived into the river. The water was icy cold, and for a second she stopped thinking. Then she started to swim down. It didn't take long to find the cart, and she grabbed onto the spokes of a wheel, using it to pull herself around. Soon the problem became clear. The man, unconscious or possibly dead already, was trapped under the cart by a wheel.

Lungs burning, she pulled herself across to him and tried to lift the vehicle. It gave a tiny bit, but as soon as she reached for the man, the weight was too much and she had to let it drop again. Moving closer, she made a second attempt. Managing to lift it further, she grabbed his collar and attempted to drag him across the riverbed, but still couldn't move him. Frustrated, she used the last of her strength to shove the cart up once again, but lost her footing and slipped forward, landing on her back. She just managed to keep hold of the edge of the cart, which was perilously close to falling and trapping her beneath it. Her lungs and arms screamed in protest. She couldn't move without risking death, but staying there was certain to have the same effect. She expelled the last of the air in her lungs with a scream of anger. The unfairness of the situation hit her all at once. She closed her eyes and prepared to let go, willing to take the quicker death of being crushed over drowning.

Suddenly, some of the weight was lifted. Mac opened her eyes. Her vision was blurred by the water and oxygen deprivation, but there was another figure there, with blonde hair floating around her face. Sola Austin grabbed Mac's collar and tugged her violently. Coming to her senses, she scrambled out from under the cart, and, barely thinking, dragged the unconscious man away while Austin held the vehicle. With barely the energy to swim, she wasn't sure she could drag him to the surface, but once again, Austin took care of it, grabbing the man, who was heavy even underwater, and shoving Mac upwards. Natural buoyancy did most of the work, although she flailed a little to speed it up, bursting to the surface and gasping desperately for air. Austin soon appeared beside her, but didn't stop, and began dragging the body into shore.

Exhausted, Mac forced herself to follow. Back on land, it seemed obvious that the man was dead. She swore violently, hating that she had gone through that for nothing, and looked up to the Spitfire, where Tristan was lowering a ladder for them.

She turned to see Austin bent over the body, with her cheek to his face. Austin then opened his mouth and put hers against it, not in a kiss, but blowing air from her to him.

"What are you doing?"

The other girl ignored her, continuing solidly at her work. The crowd that had gathered were all watching in fascination and confusion – and in the case of the woman Mac assumed was his wife, hope.

After a minute or so of this strange procedure, Mac heard a choking noise. The man began to splutter and cough violently, and Austin pushed him up into a sitting position, and slapped his back repeatedly. Water dribbled from his mouth, and eventually his breathing calmed down. His wife gasped and rushed to his side.

"He could get sick," Austin said, though the words were falling on deaf ears. "He was in there a long time."

"Thank you," the woman said, wide-eyed. "You brought him back to life."

Austin shrugged modestly.

"He wasn't quite dead yet."

But she had lost her audience, the woman was by her husband's side, holding him up and sobbing.

Mac couldn't do anything but stare at her in shock. Austin looked at the couple and smiled, then walked over.

"Shall we get back on board?"

Having said that, she was already climbing. Mac shook her head in disbelief and followed. When she reached the deck, the crew was applauding, with Austin laughing at them. Slowly, she began to clap as well. The other girl turned around in mild shock.

Mac smiled, and stretched out her hand.

CHAPTER TWENTY-FOUR

I have been living aboard this airship for far too long. I have an innate understanding now of the social complexities and undercurrents that go on. Which is why I knew, when Mackenzie Sheridan reached out her hand to me, it was big. That she had done so in front of the crew gave me an opportunity to reject it publicly – and so score a few points in this ridiculous game we have played.

But I think I am ready to move on from that now. And I think – in fact I know – that she is too. She offered her respect, and that is something I doubted I would ever get from her. I must admit, I have wanted it. She already had mine, though it was begrudgingly given.

I shook her hand.

Of course I did.

When Sola went down to the galley the following morning, the captain was already there, boiling water.

"Morning, Austin," she said with a nod of acknowledgement. "Coffee?"

Immediately, Sola liked how sounded – 'Austin' – it wasn't quite the familiar 'Sola' the rest had adopted so quickly, but Mac had at last dropped the title of 'Lady', which she had always sneered as though Sola were personally responsible for her lineage.

"Austin?" Mac repeated, breaking into her train of thought.

Sola took a second to remember the question.

"Oh! Coffee. Yes, please."

Mac stretched to a higher cupboard to retrieve a mug. It was the first time Sola had really noticed how short the captain was: a mix of good posture and authority had always hidden it well.

"Lynch tells me he's sorted your shooting problem."

"Well, hopefully." I haven't tried the gun with the new grip yet."

Mac looked thoughtful.

"Let me know how it goes," she said, handing Sola a mug.

"Are you interested in the differences between left- and right-handed guns?" Sola asked, vaguely surprised as she knew the captain didn't show much interest in Ethan's work.

"No," Mac replied, with a quiet laugh, "but my father was fascinated. Maybe part of me feels I should still be pretending to care."

"Why did you never get into the inventing thing?"

She laughed.

"It takes a certain type of brain I just don't have."

"So just the open sky for you," Sola smiled.

"Exactly."

"It's not a bad life."

"You should have been around in the good days."

She looked up quizzically.

"Is something wrong with these days?"

"You mean aside from people trying to kill us for no apparent reason? The crew is too small. It was small even with Henry and James, it's barely going to be manageable without Gloria."

"Why was it small before?" she asked.

"I laid off everyone I wasn't sure I could trust," Mac said, and snorted derisively. "Obviously my judgment was far from perfect"

She felt slightly guilty – Mac hadn't said as much, but it was obvious that the reason she'd cut down on crew was because of Sola. Then she shook herself out of it. After all she hadn't *asked* to be kidnapped, even if it was for her own safety.

"What are we going to do after Gloria leaves then?"

Mac eyed her critically

"Can you keep your mouth shut for a while? Even with Ethan?"

She nodded quickly, feeling a thrill of inclusion that reminded her of sharing secrets back in school.

"I'm thinking of going abroad for a while. The continent. We can pick up some foreign crew, they won't know who you are."

"Sorry to put you to so much trouble, Captain," Sola said, her tone light, although she was only half joking.

Fittingly, Mac laughed half-heartedly.

"Spain's nice this time of year," she said. "It's where Father taught me to swim, actually."

"Warmer than where I learnt," Sola grinned. "The lake by our country house. It's my favourite place in the world though, especially at night."

"A childhood of midnight swims, Austin?" Mac said, smirking.

"Sometimes," Sola laughed. "When we hadn't had visitors for a while. Summers with just Aunt Judith for company could be stifling."

"Interesting person, your aunt."

"Not really," Sola grumbled, though she did feel a twinge of guilt at how worried Judith must be.

"I would have thought she'd have great stories from Africa," Mac said.

Sola stopped in shock.

"Africa?"

"When I was looking into your family I heard she'd spent some time across there," Mac said, shrugging.

"She's never spoken to me about it."

"Hmm. Odd. Anyway, enjoy your breakfast. I have the joys of accounting to return to."

She left Sola in a state of complete confusion. Her aunt had never been an open person, but not to mention something as massive as this? Even once? She would have loved to hear stories from Africa. She'd love to *go* to Africa. Maybe that was a suggestion to put to Mac, if they were going to leave Britain. She laughed aloud at the thought of that conversation, and then took her breakfast up to eat in the lounge.

On one side of the table was a newspaper. Realising how long it had been since she read one, she pulled it over and checked the date. It was from the previous week, when they were in Glasgow. No wonder she hadn't noticed, with everything that had happened since. She sipped her coffee and flicked through. Most of it was pretty standard, but one page caught her eye. The headline was "London's Burning", but it wasn't the picture that sent a chill through her. She recognised the building, even in flames. Jesse had taken her there, it was another anarchist hideout. She hurriedly scanned the article, recognizing several other addresses among those that had recently burned down. Five people were dead – no names given. Her heart stopped.

Grabbing the paper, she ran along the corridor and catapulted into Mac's study.

"We need to go to London."

"What?"

"We need to go back to London. We have to go back."

Mac stood up.

"Austin, get control of yourself. What the hell are you talking about? Go back? That's the most dangerous thing we could do!"

"Look at this!"

She walked over to the desk and slammed down the paper. Mac scanned the page quickly and looked back at her.

"I don't understand."

"I..." Sola forced herself to breathe. "It's an anarchist building. They all are. Someone's killing them."

Mac spread her hands in a gesture that plainly read 'so what'.

"Someone's trying to kill *us*, Austin. It's you I promised to protect."

"These are my friends! They were... Jesse..."

Mac's eyes lit in understanding.

"You love him. Christ, don't tell Carlisle."

"For god's sake!" Sola snapped. "What about Marcus?"

"What?" Mac said sharply.

"Marcus Tate. He's your lover, isn't he? And they stay in his bloody guesthouse, didn't you know? It won't be long before that gets burned to the ground!"

Mac stopped dead. She sank back down into her chair.

"I did know," she said. "The question is how do you know about Marcus and I?"

"I read your log," Sola admitted with a twinge of guilt, but refusing to be distracted, "while you weren't on board. That's really not the point here, people are in danger and we can do something to help them. You saved me, you can save them, Captain, *please*."

"Get out," the captain said.

"You've got to listen to me..."

"Get *out*," she repeated.

But Sola was too far gone to pay any attention to the dangerous look in Captain Sheridan's eyes.

"I know you don't like the anarchists. But they're not bad people, they've just had hard lives, surely you understand?" she continued to plead. "And if you won't do it for them, and you won't do it for me, do it for Marcus!"

Mac stood again.

"*Lady Austin*. Get out of my study this instant."

"Will you take me or not? Because I'll bloody go on my own."

"Leave!"

With one last, desperate stare, Sola span on her heel and strode out of the door.

CHAPTER TWENTY-FIVE

I don't know what to think. I should protect Austin, that's all I've been trying to do. But Marcus... he's my best friend, he's... he just means too much to me. I can't get my thoughts straight. She was in here yelling, and I just wanted to shout back. Of course I want to go to bloody London and save him but it's putting you *back in the jaws of the lion you stupid, stupid girl.*

She's not actually that stupid, she just obviously cares for Jesse Armitage. Why, I can't imagine. The man sounds highly unpleasant, but then I only have the story of him blackmailing Marcus to go on. It will be a blow for Ethan if he finds out why we're going back, and he will... see now I'm writing as though I've already made my decision.

Going abroad was such a good plan. It dealt with everything, in the short term. But really there is no point in pretending I'm still trying to decide, is there?

Mac stared at the newspaper still on the table. For all she knew, the guesthouse had already been attacked. It felt as though something was slithering around in the pit of her stomach, and she knew the feeling wouldn't go away until she saw Marcus again, saw that he was safe and well with her own two eyes. And hell, if she had to save the bloody anarchists she'd do that too.

She waited until dinner to speak to the crew, when they were all gathered around the table in the lounge.

"Guys, I have a bit of an announcement to make."

"Don't tell me you're pregnant too, Captain," Rob said, grinning.

She laughed, grateful for his humour.

"No, MacKinnon. After we leave Gloria in Birmingham, we're

going to fly back to London."

"Isn't that a bit dangerous?" Ethan said, frowning in confusion.

"Yes," Mac replied simply. "I... someone is burning down all the buildings the anarchists use there. Now you know I couldn't care less about the anarchists but..."

"Marcus," said Gloria immediately.

"Exactly. He's one of my oldest friends, I can't not try."

"Friends, sure," said Tristan, smirking.

"Shut up. Look, I'm telling you now because if anyone wants to bow out, I'm happy to let you off in Birmingham. You'll get two months pay, an amazing reference, and absolutely no hard feelings. Don't say anything right now, but have a think about it and come see me later. This *will* be dangerous."

She left the room, knowing they would want to discuss this twist in her absence. Within a few seconds, Austin was in the corridor behind her.

"Thank you."

"Don't think for a second I'm doing this for them or you. It's like you said... it's for Marcus."

Sola nodded.

"I know that. I meant thank you for not telling them about my involvement."

"For not telling *him*, you mean."

"Yes."

Mac looked at her seriously.

"I don't want to break the poor man's heart. Perhaps you ought to have a think about what happens if Armitage is alive and suddenly they're in the same room, both thinking you're theirs."

"I'm not anyone's," Austin responded immediately.

She smiled a little.

"Maybe. But my point still stands."

"It does. And I... I'll tell him," Austin said firmly. "It's all in the past anyway."

"I've got to tell you, it doesn't look that way to me right now."

With that, she walked away. She wanted to be alone with a book and a glass of whiskey, and no decisions to make.

CHAPTER TWENTY-SIX

I don't know why I said I'd tell Ethan. Except that I think it is the right thing to do. That doesn't make it the easiest thing to do, though – far from it. I do think of everything with Jesse as being in the past, but obviously it's unresolved at the same time. And I'm not just willing to sit back and wait for him to die when I could have done something to prevent it. Even if it is at the cost of seemingly having reversed any progress Captain Sheridan and I had made.

And even if it is at the cost of Ethan and I's relationship I suppose. I love him, but is love worth a life? Any life? I don't know. I don't know anything. I have to do what I think is right, and hope it turns out for the best. I hope he will forgive me.

Sola had never walked more slowly from her cabin to the workshop. When she knocked the door, there was no reply.

"Ethan?" she called quietly.

When there was still silence, she wondered if he was still eating in the lounge. However, something told her otherwise. After big revelations he tended to retreat and think about things. He would be inside. Which meant he didn't want to speak to her.

"I'm coming in now," she said. "Shout and stop me if it's dangerous."

Again, nothing. She cracked the door open as little as possible and stepped inside. He looked up from his workbench.

"This didn't come from Mac," he said. "She wants to save Marcus, but it wasn't her idea."

"No."

"No one else will work it out because they don't know about you and those bloody anarchists. See this was my problem all along – *you* putting yourself in danger for those idiots. And now you're putting other people in danger too!"

She breathed in sharply.

"They can leave," she said defensively.

"They *won't* though," he replied. "They're loyal, they will throw themselves into this for Mac. Or at least, they think they're doing it for her."

"You don't think they'd do it for me?"

He sighed.

"You know, I actually think they would. Does that make it better or worse that you're doing this to them?"

"The anarchists are my friends too, Ethan," she said softly. "I wouldn't abandon the crew if they were in danger, I won't abandon them either."

"What have they ever done for you to gain this loyalty?"

"Jesse was always good to me," she said immediately.

"Jesse Armitage?" he asked.

"Yes. How do you know?"

"I've stayed at Marcus', I know the regular guests. It's him you're doing this for then?"

From the look in his eyes, she could tell that he'd made the connection.

"It's not like that," she said weakly.

"Tell me what it is like then."

"We were together. Once, one night. And I do... I did care about him. I can't just leave him to be killed, please understand."

"Oh, I understand," he said, voice heavy with sarcasm.

"Don't be like that, Ethan."

He scowled. Sola felt a flare of anger in her chest.

"Leave in Birmingham if you have that much objection," she said harshly. "Otherwise, accept that you are a part of this crew and this is what they are doing and get on with it."

He laughed bitterly.

"Are you trying for captain now, Lady Austin? Operating from behind the scenes, pulling the strings..."

"I don't think that Captain Sheridan would appreciate you calling her a puppet," she replied, stung by the use of her title.

"It's how she's behaving!"

"Oh so being angry at me isn't enough, you're going to be angry at her now, really mature of you."

"And putting everyone in danger to rescue some murderous anarchist you had sex with once is mature, is it?"

She gasped.

"Yes, actually. Yes it bloody is, because it's the right thing to do!"

"I can't believe you think that."

"I can't believe you don't. You know you could save lives but you don't even want to *try*. I thought you were better than that."

"Sola, I..."

"What?"

"Nothing. Never mind."

"Grow up, Ethan."

She couldn't think of any way it could have gone worse. She was equal parts furious and upset, and once she was out of the workshop, she ran back up to her cabin and threw herself onto the bed. Unable to control herself, she sobbed into the pillow. She hadn't meant it to be about love, or relationships, or any of that. She was just trying to get by and make a life for herself and make decisions she would be able to live with. It would be so much easier with Ethan's support though. Remembering his accusations of selfishness just made her burn up with anger again though, and she refused to apologise when she honestly believed that she was in the right.

Part of Sola wanted to get to London as soon as possible, part of her wanted to delay it. Correspondingly, the journey seemed to go quickly some days and slower others. The leg to Birmingham was fast. Watching Gloria hug her brother on the docks had been emotional, as she then proceeded to hug each of them in turn. Predictably, neither Rob nor Tristan had taken up the offer of leaving. She wondered if Ethan would, but he stayed.

From that point on, flying the Spitfire was even more difficult. They all needed to work all day. Ethan didn't have time to be in his workshop much, which was awkward, as they weren't speaking to each other. Some nights Sola had gone up on deck to think, and seen Mac at the wheel, frantically trying to speed up the movements of the ship and keep it on track on her own. Things were still frosty with the captain as well, but she could understand the complaint there. She had read what was essentially Mac's diary, and then exploited her relationship to openly manipulate her. Her behaviour had been out of line, but she hadn't been able to see another way.

At least Mac was making an effort to be civil. Ethan was nothing but cold. How things had changed since her first day on the Spitfire!

Her life consisted of working, sleeping, and worrying about everything. One day, an eternity later and yet still too soon, the silhouette of London appeared on the horizon against the rising sun.

"There by tonight," said Mac. "Is everyone ready?"

Grimly, the tiny, fractured crew of the Spitfire nodded.

CHAPTER TWENTY-SEVEN

I am exhausted, but it is a good exhaustion this time. It is the exhaustion of having worked hard to achieve something, and having nearly succeeded. I will not count it as a victory until I have Marcus in my arms, but I can feel that we are near.

The past several days have been far from pleasant. Even if we were all getting on, it would have been bloody hard work, but with Ethan and Austin not speaking, and myself not quite able to forgive Austin for this whole thing (though I do see her reasons, and I will get there eventually) it has been uncomfortable in every possible way.

There was a knock on her door.

"Come in."

When she saw who it was, her eyes widened in surprise.

"Ethan, you don't usually visit me."

"I wanted to have a last-ditch attempt at making you change your mind, Captain."

"Well, at least you're upfront about your intentions," she said lightly.

"Captain..."

"I can't, Ethan," she said, genuinely hurting for him. "I can't."

"I know you love him, Mac-"

"I don't..." she trailed off. "It doesn't matter."

"But I love her," Ethan persisted. "I really do. And I just want to keep her safe, please, London isn't safe for her. Those anarchists aren't safe for her and I'm not just saying that because..."

"You're jealous?" Mac supplied.

"I am," he admitted. "Of course I am! Maybe I shouldn't be, I don't know. But that's not why, Captain, I promise you, I'm just trying to keep her safe."

"Ethan... if you love her, make her feel like she has your support. That's what she needs from you right now, not a bodyguard."

"I don't support this."

She ran her hand through her hair.

"I understand, Ethan. But I need to see Marcus. I need to know he's safe. Please don't... I know you're disappointed in me."

He didn't deny it. With a sigh, he left the room. She rested her head in her hands. Every time she thought things couldn't get worse, something else seemed to fall apart. She went out onto the back deck for fresh air, to look out at the setting sun, and then saw how close they were getting to the city, and ran up the stairs to the main deck to steer. She didn't want to head for the docks this time; she was going directly to her destination. It was hard to navigate London from birds-eye view as the day darkened, but she did her best, bringing the ship far lower than regulations technically allowed. A few people in the city below looked up, but she ignored it, desperately searching out the familiar street. Then something caught in her throat, and she began to cough.

It was smoke.

She span around, and spotted it just a few streets behind them – a massive blaze. Spinning the wheel as fast as possible, the ship banked onto its side at a threateningly steep angle before straightening in the right direction. It had the added bonus of bringing everyone running to the deck. They all started working the ropes, and the Spitfire took off towards the burning building. A closer look confirmed her worst fear – it was the guesthouse.

She threw down a mooring anchor, which clattered against the street, eventually catching on a lamppost and bringing the ship to a sudden halt. Tristan already had the ladder over the side and was most of the way down it, she went for the direct approach of climbing over the railing and stretching across to a tiny balcony by one of the windows. The bars were hot, burning the leather of her gloves, but she managed to keep her bare fingers from touching the metal. She was hit by a wall of heat, but forced herself to press on, climbing through the window and plunging into the inferno. The room was empty, so she pressed out into the hall and ran to where there was screaming from the far room. There was a wall of fire by the door. Hesitating for only a second, she sprinted through it, feeling her clothes light.

Suddenly, something heavy and dark was over her. She fought her way out of it, to discover her clothes had been put out.

"What the fuck did you do that for?" someone yelled at her. "Get out!"

She realised whoever it was had thrown a blanket over her to douse the flames, and tried to look at them through the heat-haze and smoke.

"Marcus!"

"Mac?!"

"Thank god you're alive, let's go!"

But she soon saw the problem – two women, one of who had a small child in her arms. She pulled out a gun and shot the window. It shattered. The rush of air fuelled the fire, which billowed outwards.

"Give me the child," she yelled.

Neither the bawling toddler nor his mother did anything. Frustrated, she grabbed the boy, who to her relief, clenched his arms around his neck. She climbed with as much care as possible out of the window, still managing to scratch herself to pieces on the glass. Shuffling along the sill was difficult with a child on her chest, but she managed and then twisted around to sit on it. The boy cried louder – she guessed he'd just looked down. The Spitfire was too far away to reach from this window... for her. She saw Lynch on board the deck, helping soot covered strangers.

"Tristan!" she screamed.

Within seconds, the man was scaling the wall with seemingly impossible skill.

"Put him over my shoulder," he said urgently.

"You've got to stay still," she told the child, who kept screaming. "Calm the *fuck* down."

The expletive silenced him immediately, which would have been funny in any other situation.

"Stay very still," she said again, and unpeeled him from her neck, still holding him tightly.

It was difficult, but she managed to get the boy over Tristan's shoulders, hanging still – either following her instructions or paralysed by fear. Tristan scrambled back along the wall and climbed back onto the ship. She watched, holding her breath until the boy was safely on deck.

Then she steeled herself to go back in. Turning round, Marcus and the two women were staring from the window. The fire was swallowing up the room quickly.

"Tristan won't be able to carry us along that, we'll have to go through the fire."

"I have plenty of blankets, we'll wrap ourselves in them," Marcus said, and burst into a fit of coughing. He struggled through, throwing a heavy wool swathe of material at each of them in turn.

Following his advice, Mac drew hers around herself. The four of them looked oddly comical, and she was struck with a bizarre desire to laugh. Then Marcus started, running in the blaze. Refusing to think about it, she followed.

There were pockets of brief respite – where the air was stiflingly hot and suffocating, but not actually yet alight, and the trip was mostly a case of running full pelt through the flames, stumbling into each beautiful oasis. Mac kept a vague eye on the figure of Marcus – oddly shaped due to the blanket and distorted by the flames. At last they stumbled out into the street and fell to the ground. Mac threw off the blanket, and gasped for air, drinking in the fresh air around her. The other women soon followed out of the fire. She glanced over at Marcus, also kneeling in the filthy street, and caught his eye.

Inexplicably, they started to laugh. It went from a chuckle to full-blown hysteria, and the two women joined in. Trying desperately to gain some measure of control over herself, Mac looked up at the Spitfire to see several soot covered strangers on the deck. More were on the ground, waiting to climb up, as were her crew.

Sola Austin was desperately questioning every stranger.

"Have you seen Jesse? Jesse Armitage? Is he still in there?"

She was met mostly with shrugs and noncommittal grunts.

"I've got to-" she started running towards the building.

Mac tried to stand and go after her, but Ethan was there in an instant, shoving her back and away from the fire.

"*Don't*," he said. A second passed, and he shook his head. "Wait here."

Barely flinching, he ran head on into the inferno. Austin screamed his name and flung herself after him, but this time Mac managed to get onto her feet, and grab the girl's arm. Marcus was soon beside her, holding back the other arm as Austin lost all control, thrashing desperately to get away from them. They held firm, waiting until the fit passed, and even then, reluctant to let go.

"There's no point you both going," Mac said. "There's no point, Austin. He did it to protect you."

This was evidently the wrong thing to say, as she wailed in response and began to sob uncontrollably. Mac judged it was safe to let go at that point, and sure enough, Austin didn't try to run again, but nor would she move from that point. She had to fight the urge to run after Carlisle herself – and when he returned, she was going to berate him for being so bloody stupid. But she knew he'd done it to keep Austin safe, and wasn't about to let her ruin that.

They waited in silence after Austin's sobs died away. The building was far from quiet though. Walls and ceilings were caving in and crashing. Every dreadful noise worried her a little more.

Then two men emerged, their limping, stumbling forms silhouetted against the fierce light of the fire. Ethan wasn't one of them. They were both stockier, a little shorter. As they got closer, Mac saw one of them had short brown hair and a strong, defined face. Good looking if it weren't for the soot that marked every inch of skin, and the massive, shining burn down one side of his chest. He barely seemed alive.

The other, she recognised instantly, even if his blonde hair was covered in a coating of ash, and his blue eyes were shining with tears. It was James.

"Is Ethan...?" she heard herself whisper, not even aware of choosing to say the words.

"The man who saved my life?" the newcomer croaked, his throat clearly parched by the heat.

James shook his head, the tears falling freely from his eyes.

"The floor fell. I tried..." his eyes shifted elsewhere, staring blankly out of his face. "I tried," he repeated softly, to himself.

Mac heard a wail of horror, but didn't know if it was Austin's or her own.

CHAPTER TWENTY-EIGHT

This was entirely my fault. It was all me. I did this to him. I can't believe I did this. I shouldn't have let him go in there. Why did I let him? I could have stopped him, surely I could have stopped him. I should have just listened to him. Jesse is safe. Injured, but safe, being treated in the galley with the rest. But Ethan is dead. My god, dead. He's actually gone. He was the only person... he loved me, I know he did, and I treated him so badly. I read back to my stubborn refusal to apologise, to make any form of peace... why did I do that? Why was my pride more important than making peace? He loved me. I loved him, and I may as well have killed him. If I'd known... if I could take it back... if I could just say sorry. I'm so sorry. I'm so sorry. Ethan please don't do this to me, I don't want to do this without you. I'm not even sure that I can. You made me feel so wanted, respected, desired, so loved, and you didn't want anything from me except that I put my own safety first. And I ignored you, and I killed you, and I'm so sorry.

Sola let her pen clatter to the floor. What was the point of it, anyway? Writing about it wasn't going to make her feel better. The opposite – seeing it there in ink, 'Ethan is dead', made everything worse. Why had she written that? What was she thinking? She went to lie on the bed, wanting to just fall asleep and never wake up again, but she had a fleeting image of him lying on that same bed, illuminated by the morning sun. She ran into the en suite and threw up. Head hanging over the toilet bowl, she waited to cry, but there were no tears left in her. She didn't remember anything after James' whisper of "I tried", but she knew she had totally lost it. Her throat hurt from the screaming.

If she couldn't avoid memories of Ethan, she could do the opposite.

It would hurt, but really, she deserved the pain. Forcing herself to stand, she left the cabin and walked down to the workshop, and for the first time, straight in. His presence hit her like a wall. The room hadn't changed, it didn't know. His belongings were scattered, papers with his rough working were everywhere, as though waiting for him to return and finish the calculations.

She wasn't ready to act otherwise, so she collapsed into her usual seat and stared blankly around the room. She'd wanted something to present itself down here, for it to give her some clarity of reason, but there was nothing, just the same endless emptiness. She left again. Head down, she bumped straight into someone coming out of the gallery.

"Shit!"

The violence of the exclamation made her look up. It was Jesse, and she had bumped into his burnt side. His face was screwed up in agony. When he saw who it was though, he stopped in his tracks.

"Sola?"

She couldn't meet his eye.

"Oh my god, Sola, we've been so worried about you. We thought something had happened because of what you've been doing for us, we were worried sick..."

"I'm fine," she whispered, despite how obviously untrue it was.

He reached to tilt her chin upwards, but she flinched away from his touch. She could feel the confusion emanating from him, but couldn't explain.

"I'm glad you're alive," she managed to say, though that wasn't completely true either.

Then, totally disregarding courtesy, she turned and practically fled upstairs. Up on deck, Mac was steering.

The captain looked deadly. She hadn't washed or changed, still clung to by soot. The only parts of her skin that weren't totally black were the mucky trails from her eyes, which had now been dried in the wind. Her hair was loose and set flying, and she commanded the ship with a thoughtless confidence and total control. Sola felt a pang of jealousy. How was she holding herself together? How did she keep going? She didn't approach. She knew she would need to speak to Mac at some point, but couldn't face it just yet.

Instead she turned to the rigging, and Mac's secret came to her in an instant – she kept going because she was focusing on something purely physical. She grasped the ropes and began to climb. For the first time, she wasn't thinking about her footholds or her next move. Her arms burned in that familiar way, and she welcomed it, pulling herself further and further up. She was not frightened of falling anymore. She wasn't planning on throwing herself from the ropes, but if it happened, if she fell, she wouldn't mind. Eventually, the exertion managed to drive all thoughts away, leaving the emptiness, the persistent guilt, but mostly just a heart beating faster and muscles protesting the activity. She was disappointed when she reached the crow's nest and looked out across the city. Even momentary stillness gave the thoughts time to return.

Giving up, she curled into a ball within the basket and waited, allowing the three demons of her mind – Memories, Hindsight and Shame – to torture her.

Sola came down when she needed water. The sun had already set by this point, and everyone was inside the ship. The chances of navigating her way around the Spitfire without being seen were small. There were more people around than usual. She kept her eyes fixed on the ground, collected water from the galley, and retreated back to her room. Thankfully, conversation wasn't a priority for anybody. It didn't take her long to finish the water – she hadn't realised how thirsty she was. But, with that thirst quenched, another rose in her. Was having to speak to Mac worth the trouble? She remembered the burn of whiskey searing down her throat, and stood. It was high time she faced the music anyway.

She didn't knock, knowing Mac wouldn't want to receive visitors, and would probably pretend not to be in.

"Austin," was the cold greeting. "How are you?"

"How do you think I am?" Sola croaked.

"I honestly don't know."

"I want to die," Sola said.

"Please don't," Mac replied. "It would defeat the purpose of his death completely."

"This is my fault."

"Yes, it is."

Despite having blamed herself, Mac's agreement angered her.

"Though it was him who chose to go in there," she qualified. "I didn't want him to."

"He did it to stop you from doing the same thing," Mac said. "He died for you."

"He died saving Jesse..." she said, but she knew what was coming, and that it was true.

"You think he gave a damn about Armitage?"

"No," Sola whispered. "Do you think I'm not blaming myself already? Do you think I *wanted* this to happen?"

"I don't *know* what to think! Do you understand that? I have no earthly *idea* what to think. I know Ethan loved you, I know that. I know you were with him but you were also with this Armitage guy, I know you *begged* me and manipulated me to come and save him-"

"Are you not glad you did?!" Sola shouted back at her. "Are you not happy at all that *your* lover is *alive* because of me? Marcus is alive, and Ethan is dead, how come you get to be angry?!"

"Because Armitage is alive too! I have no idea what Ethan meant to you, I don't know if he was just a fling, if you were just passing the time, but he was *in love with you* and now he's dead and your old flame is alive because of it so I don't know what to think, and yes, I do get to be fucking angry!"

"What makes you think I wasn't in love with him too?"

"Well were you?"

"Yes!"

The word was out of her mouth in an instant, and as soon as she said it, she knew it was true. She was totally in love with Ethan: something far more real and strong than the infatuation she had had with Jesse.

Mac deflated. Immediately it was clear that her anger had been a coping mechanism, and nothing more.

"Sit down, Sola," she said tiredly.

And then, as Sola had predicted, she made her way over to the drawers and pulled out the whiskey.

"What a mess," the captain said, as she poured the drinks and carried them across to the table. "I've dropped everyone not wanted by the police off at a hospital, incidentally. You might have missed that while you were hiding up in your little nest."

"You saw me then?"

"I saw you start climbing," she said. "From there it was pretty obvious where you'd be."

"The anarchists are all still on board?"

It was obvious she was only asking about one person.

"Those who aren't well known went to the hospital. Armitage, and the two women, Wraith and Gainsbury are still onboard, as is Gainsbury's son. And Marcus is still here as well."

"Where are they sleeping?"

It was a ridiculous question, but Sola wanted to stay focused on trivial details.

"Marcus is in Henry's cabin, Gainsbury and the boy are in Gloria's. Armitage and Wraith are in the crew quarters."

"Charity and Eleanor could share, you know," said Sola lightly.

Mac gave her a confused look.

"It's not like there isn't plenty space in the crew room..."

Sola chuckled. The noise shocked her, and she immediately went quiet.

"What's so funny?" said Mac, tactfully ignoring it.

"I meant they might prefer to share," Sola replied, her voice heavy with significance.

There was a moment of silence.

"Oh. Ohh."

"Yeah."

"I see."

"Yes."

"I missed that."

"They hide it well."

Sola couldn't prevent another smile into her whiskey glass.

"Though I am hoping they aren't planning on staying much longer, so it shouldn't matter."

"What about Marcus?"

Mac shook her head.

"I've been trying to convince him for years, but he won't leave London. His sister was bought by a family from here, he's made finding her his life's mission since he escaped."

"He was a slave?"

"What did you think?" she said with a disbelieving look.

"I don't know. He's just so..."

"Proud," Mac finished softly. "Yes, I know. He escaped when he was fifteen. When we found him, in Wales, he'd been caught and was being publicly whipped."

"No..."

"Father bought him. He would have given him a job, a paid one, but Marcus didn't want to work on airships. He just wanted to find his sister. So we brought him to London."

"And so began a long and complicated relationship?"

"You have no idea. But then, that was how James chose to come here. He said that he knew eventually I'd visit Marcus again," she said, choking up a little even as she laughed.

They fell into silence again, having exhausted the avenue of vaguely light conversation that was preventing them from discussing Ethan. Sola steeled herself for further confrontation when Mac next spoke.

"I wanted to ask about your locket."

She hadn't been expecting that.

"What about it?"

"It has a dragonfly on it. Why?"

"My mother liked them. I think it's because of the lake at the country house – remember I told you? In the evening the dragonflies all fly low over the water – clouds of them. It's stunning. They're incredible."

"That explains it then."

"Explains what?"

Mac stood and walked over to her desk. Back to Sola, she began to speak.

"I went down to Ethan's workshop. Just to have a look around. I don't really know why, I'm not ready to clear it out or anything like that. But I found something he's been working on, and I couldn't think why. No practical use whatsoever."

The Spitfire Project

Sola heard a click and the spinning of gears, and then something that resembled the beating of wings. Mac turned and opened her cupped hands. Something silver flitted out of them and around the room a little, before perching on the table in front of Sola. It was a silver mechanical dragonfly, with blue glass eyes. Captivated, she reached out her hand. The animal (immediately, she couldn't think of it as a machine), stepped up into her palm. Laughing with delight, Sola brought it closer to examine.

"It's beautiful," she said.

"It's yours," Mac replied. "You should name it really."

She watched it fly a little, spinning in circles above her head, and grinned.

"It's called Vertigo," she said.

Mac caught her eye, and burst into laughter.

CHAPTER TWENTY-NINE

This whole thing has gotten utterly ridiculous. It's time to take a stand and find some answers. Ethan's death should have made me more cautious, more worried, but today I am feeling reckless instead. We have run away for long enough, and now we should really gain some measure of control over our lives. I have protected Austin out of loyalty to my father, but it has hardly ended well. time to move onto the offense, I think.

Having written those decisive words, Mac left her study and knocked on the door to Sola's cabin. She thought of it as Sola's now, but it had taken her some time to stop internally referring to it as her own. Now, even as she stepped in the door, she didn't feel as though it were her room.

"Where does Duke Bernard live?" she said, not bothering with niceties.

"Why?" Sola asked.

"It's time to get some bloody answers, Austin, I'm sick of not knowing anything."

It was slightly worrying that Sola's face lit up instantly.

"I'll take you there."

Mac thought about arguing, but only momentarily.

"Brilliant. Let's go."

"Now?"

"Now."

The Spitfire was busy enough that nobody noticed them stringing the rope ladder from the back balcony and climbing down onto the docks. Mac's heart was beating from the adrenaline already, and it felt incredible. They walked briskly from the industrial areas of the city, getting into gradually more affluent streets. Eventually they were among huge townhouses. Sola stopped in front of one.

"This is it," she announced. "How are we going to get in?"

"Oh, that part's easy enough, you'll find," Mac laughed, remembering the night of the kidnap.

She led Sola around to the kitchen door, which was wedged open, with a scullery maid smoking beside it. She gave them a suspicious look. Mac slipped a coin into her hand, far more than the favour was truly worth. The maid pretended to consider the offer for a few seconds.

"Ten minutes," she whispered, and walked inside.

Sola followed in mute shock, although the mute part didn't last long.

"That is *scary*."

"Oh come on, you already know we managed to kidnap you. Did you think it took master criminals?"

"Now you mention it, you guys are kind of stupid."

"Oh shut up. Come on, I don't know the layout of these places. Where do we go?"

Sola smirked.

"Remembering that I've snooped around this house before, I can take you directly to the mysterious document that probably started the whole thing."

"I knew I kept you around for a reason, Austin."

They emerged from the servant stairs into a lavish hall, which Sola led her through with confidence. Up another elaborate staircase and down a long corridor, they reached an oak door. Sola reached for the handle.

"Wait," Mac whispered, remembering her mistake from the Bingley's ship.

She lightly tapped on the wood. There was silence.

"Go ahead."

Looking at her strangely, Sola continued. The study wasn't unlike Mac's own, though lacking a mezzanine to sleep on. Sola immediately headed around to beside the desk and opened a drawer, pulling out a thick file full of papers. She glanced at the first page, and nodded.

"This is it," she said softly.

Mac grabbed the file, and immediately saw a detail she wished Sola had remembered earlier.

The page was headed: "The Spitfire Project". The rest was as she had described – engineering diagrams that meant absolutely nothing to her. Ethan, of course, was now unable to help. The footnote read "Science: Patrick Sheridan, Organisation: Lord George Austin".

Her heart jumped at seeing her father's name. She tucked the file under her arm, wishing she'd had the foresight to bring a bag.

"We should go now."

They set off towards the door, but as Mac reached for the handle, someone opened it from the other side. She stumbled back and caught her balance, then looked at the new arrivals.

Mac assumed the man was Duke Bernard, but the she didn't recognise the gun-wielding woman behind him. Sola apparently did.

"Aunt Judith?!"

"Sola!" The woman's face lifted, illuminating her otherwise severe features. "What the hell happened to you?"

"I could ask the same!" Sola said in shock. "You have a gun?"

"Of course I have a gun, silly girl. Did you think I relied on other people to protect me?"

Mac slowly reached for the weapon at her own hip, but Sola's aunt swung the barrel towards her.

"Don't you dare, I don't know you or why you're here. You, Bernard, take a seat."

The duke, glancing between the three women in the room, slowly made his way over to his chair and collapsed into it.

"Well I think the only real question here is who should explain themselves first," Mac said.

Judith Austin looked at her scathingly.

"Given which one of us has a gun drawn, young lady, I'd say you."

"The appropriate title would be 'Captain'," Mac said, holding back a smirk. How could Sola say this woman was boring?

"Captain of what?"

"The airship named the Spitfire."

The woman's eyes widened.

"You're Patrick and Aislin's daughter," she said immediately.

"You knew my parents?"

"Only a little. Through their friendship with my brother and his wife. Well that explains why you're here – I suppose Sola found out about this whole thing somehow and ran off with you."

Mac coughed.

"It would probably be more accurate to say she was kidnapped, and eventually came to see that it was for her own safety. What is this whole thing, might I ask?"

"It's named after your airship, don't you know?"

Slightly embarrassed, she shook her head.

"The Spitfire Project? That means nothing to you?"

"Nothing other than I've just read it at the top of some file."

Judith turned to Sola.

"Sola, do you know what the Spitfire Project is?"

"Do you?" said Sola eagerly.

"No, of course I don't, what do you think I'm trying to figure out?"

Mac looked over at Russell Bernard, who had decided the best strategy was to sit quietly.

"I think there is only one person in this room with the answer to that," she said softly, "and a lot of other questions besides. May I suggest that we take Duke Bernard to the Spitfire? I'm not comfortable holding him in an area he knows well, and we do not, full of people he employs."

Judith eyed her critically, before giving a decisive nod.

"I have a carriage waiting outside. Your ship is at the docks?"

Judith led the way, with her gun subtly pressed into Duke Bernard's back. Sola and Mac walked behind, shooting each other looks of confusion, fear and slight amusement. The ride to the docks was undertaken in utter silence, making it feel twice as long as it really was. However, at last, they managed to get everyone aboard the Spitfire, which Mac set loose, taking them high above the city so there was no possible escape route.

The commotion had drawn the remaining members of the crew, the anarchists, and Marcus to the deck, and James articulated their feelings as they watched Judith Austin, in her large skirts and scraped back hair, bind the duke to a railing.

"Cap, sorry, but what the fuck is going on?"

"I don't know, Riddle," she said, and grinned. "But for the first time in a while, I'm able to find out."

And so she strode over to the kneeling man with his wrists bound to her ship.

"What is the Spitfire Project, Duke Bernard?"

"I want your word that I won't be harmed," was the first sentence she heard him say.

"I'm sorry?"

"I want your word that when you hear my story, neither you nor your pathetic crew will hurt me," he said firmly.

"Well, calling my crew pathetic isn't a good way to start this," she said lightly. "But what makes you think I'll be inclined to keep my word after this story of yours?"

He looked straight into her eyes.

"I knew your father," he said simply.

Looking at him, she believed it, and wanted to know how.

"Alright," she said.

"I want your *word*, Captain Sheridan."

"You have it, now speak."

Glancing to the side, she realised Judith Austin was looking at her with a grudging respect.

"The Spitfire Project was an idea. To build a fleet of light, fast aircraft – not airships, no balloon. Streamlined, efficient... glorious. I don't understand the mechanics. Patrick did all that. It would have transformed the infrastructure of the world. It was revolutionary."

"How were my parents involved?" Sola asked.

"George was a visionary," he said. "He got through all the legal hoops, kept them up and running, organized meetings with interested parties – and when the government pulled its support, he began to fund the project himself. I wish he hadn't. He'd be alive if he hadn't."

"Why?"

"It was revolutionary," the duke repeated. "You've got to understand, some people don't like change. Some people lose out when things change."

"Edward Bingley," Mac gasped, suddenly connecting the dots.

Duke Bernard inclined his head.

"Edward Bingley," he agreed. "My son, you've got to understand that he took my son. He made me do it."

"Made you do what?"

He looked up, and his expression was truly frightening.

"I burnt it down," he whispered hoarsely. "I burnt down the warehouse. They were all meant to die, but they escaped onto the Spitfire. Except Aislin. I watched, George went back in for her, he saved her but he..."

"He died to save her," Sola said.

She'd always known her father died in a fire, but knowing the details told her so much more about him.

"Yes, and then Aislin died in childbirth that same night," he inclined his head towards Mac. "Patrick came to see me, he was devastated. Gave me all the papers, all the evidence, everything. Said it was best if we never spoke of it again. We all agreed."

"What changed?" Judith cut in.

"Your bloody sister-in-law," he replied. "Had her baby and went nuts. Blamed Patrick, blamed me, became obsessed with finding whoever had started that fire. I'd just gotten my son back, I had to stop her before she found out too much."

"My mother committed suicide," Sola said, her tone uncertain.

"Yes," said the duke. "Like I said, she went crazy."

"That's not what you said though," Judith told him. "You said you stopped her. Dear god... Bea didn't kill herself, did she?"

And the look on the man's face said everything.

"But she was inside an asylum..." Sola said, her disbelief apparent.

"Doctors can be bought," said Judith. "Am I right?"

"Those with opium addictions can be," agreed Duke Bernard.

There was the bloody drug again, Mac thought, the smell from that cargo hold flooding back to her.

"And when you found Sola looking at that file, you panicked," Mac supplied, feeling sick to the stomach but wanting to get through the facts.

"I made my mistake," said the duke. "I wrote to Patrick. I was so *sick* of being responsible for everything. He was the one who said we should keep it quiet! I wanted him to just... deal with it, somehow."

"But he wouldn't?"

"He wrote back to me, warning me in no uncertain terms not to touch a hair on Sola Austin's head. From the way he was writing, I could tell he'd started to piece things together. I could see it was all going to fall apart. I'd put this in my past, please, understand, I'd moved on."

"You had my father killed as well," Mac said blankly, trying not to let any emotion show. "Did you plan on killing Sola?"

The duke was utterly silent, as was the whole of the crowd on the deck. Then Jesse Armitage limped forward, the top of his burn visible at his collar, the skin red and shining.

"You said you burnt it down," he said. "Is playing with fire something you do a lot of?"

"I don't understand what you're insinuating, young man."

"Your name is Russell Bernard?" Armitage said.

The man said nothing, so he looked round at Mac, who nodded in confirmation.

"You recently joined the Government's anti-anarchism 'taskforce'," he said, his scorn for the final word obvious.

"How the hell do you know that?"

Armitage gave him a scathing look.

"You joined it shortly before my safehouses started burning down, in fact. And now you confess to arson, so I'll ask once more, is playing with fire something you do a lot of?"

Bernard looked stricken. Mac felt rage grip her as she thought of Ethan, running into the flames. She forced herself to breathe and keep quiet until she gained control.

"Edward Bingley blackmailed you the first time," she said. "Which is no excuse, incidentally. Why do it again?"

But as soon as she asked the question, the answer came to her. The bombs that the anarchists had set, that had drawn so much attention to them... they had managed to kill a *few* aristocrats. The names had meant nothing to her before.

"My son," the duke said, and began to cry.

She felt no sympathy, and just stared blankly at the pathetic figure in front of her. Slowly, she reached for the pistol at her hip. His head snapped up.

"You gave me your word," he accused.

"I did," she agreed, "and you're right that my father raised me to keep it. Luckily for me, Lady Austin is not a member of my crew."

She walked over to Sola and pressed her father's gun firmly into her left hand.

"Unluckily for you, you just confessed to murdering her parents and the man she loved," she continued, and then looked directly into Sola's eyes. "Your choice," she said softly.

Mac watched, holding her breath, as Sola gripped the gun and walked slowly toward the tied duke.

"Don't do this, Lady Austin," the man said, choking on his fear. "You're better than this."

"You don't know me," replied Sola, and her voice was perfectly steady.

She lifted the weapon, holding it about a foot from his head, and fired.

CHAPTER THIRTY

You would think killing a man would make you feel something. That you would be in some way different, after that. I don't feel different at all. It's like I don't have room for anything but the permeating emptiness of Ethan's death.

I am faintly curious about how Judith got into this, but knowing that I will find out soon makes a pleasant change. Having changed and washed the blood from my skin, I suppose it is time to face people again, and to give Mac her gun, which is sitting next to me as I write.

A part of me wonders what she is doing with Duke Bernard's body, but then, so long as he is gone, I don't really care. This apathy will kill me. I shouldn't like it as much as I do.

She opened the door to find Jesse, his arm raised as though he were about to knock.

"Good afternoon," he said, a little awkwardly. He glanced down at the gun in her hand.

"I suppose you should come in," Sola replied, knowing that this conversation had been coming for quite a while.

"I think so."

She stepped back to allow him to enter, and placed the gun back down on the desk.

"I was going to return it," she explained.

"I see."

"I am going to get one though," she said defiantly.

"Captain Sheridan is dropping us off soon," he said suddenly. "I've found someone who'll take us in."

"Oh. So this is goodbye then?"

"I think so," he said again. "I wanted to thank you. She told me that it was you who wanted to save us. So thank you."

"I wish we hadn't."

"I guessed that. 'The man she loves' – that's the one who saved me, right?"

"Ethan. Yes."

"I'm very sorry, Sola. I never meant to hurt you. It seems all that I've done is put you in danger and cause you pain."

She snorted lightly.

"That's what Ethan thought as well."

"I hope it wasn't all bad," he said, smiling sadly.

Looking at him, she felt a genuine smile lifting the corners of her lips.

"It wasn't," she said. "And you did more for me than that. And I did love you, I think, but you and I could never have been together."

"You are an aristocrat," he said, laughing.

"That's not why," she replied, shaking her head. "You couldn't have loved me like I would have wanted you to. You always would have seen me as a way to gather information, to get close to the aristocracy."

To his credit, he didn't try to deny it.

"That doesn't mean I don't care at all."

"I know," she said, reaching out to hold his hand.

She marveled at the fact that he had once made her feel so young and foolish. She felt anything but young now.

"Have a doctor you trust look at that burn," she said seriously, as she caught sight of it above his collar. "It'll get infected otherwise."

He laughed.

"I will."

"I'm serious."

He squeezed her hand.

"Are you sure you won't come with us?" he said. "We'd love to have you. And not just me, and not just because of you and I."

Sola shook her head.

"I'm happier here. Not to mention I just think of Ethan when I look at you. Do you understand?"

"I do."

She ran her thumb over the back of his hand before pulling away.

"I'm going to say goodbye to Charity and Eleanor," she said, and he followed her out.

With the anarchists gone, the ship seemed empty again. Sola wandered into the crew lounge to see a sight that made her laugh aloud – her aunt having a drink with Mackenzie Sheridan.

Mac was reading something, while Judith spoke at her. Sola dragged up a chair.

"What's going on here, then?"

"I've decided I oppose strikes," said Mac, not looking up.

"I would have thought they'd be right up your street," Sola replied.

In answer, Mac slipped the paper across to her.

"Imagine if that had arrived sooner, instead of being held up by the bloody postal service."

She frowned as she saw her name at the top of the page, in unfamiliar slanting handwriting.

My dearest Sola,

I hope you will forgive the familiarity, seeing as we have never met. At your birth I was named godfather, but your mother soon changed her mind. She could not stand that I lived while George – your father – died. She blamed me for it, not without reason. It was my enthusiasm that drove the Spitfire Project on. It was my naivety to believe that we could change the world and face no consequences. So perhaps Beatrice was right to blame me. I would not blame you if you felt the same way, yet I am terrified that you do. I could say I have never contacted you for your own protection and it would be partially true, but what is also true is that I fear your condemnation. There you have it. I face down pirates but flee the judgment of a child. Though you are not a child any longer. And you have discovered something about Spitfire. Your life is under threat.

Before this, all I had to offer you were apologies for the many failings I have listed. Now I can also offer you protection. I will be in London within the next fortnight. If you wish to come with me aboard my airship, you are more than welcome, but it is your decision. Please believe the threat I have mentioned is very, very real, and close to home.

No matter your choice, though I hardly have the right to ask this of you, I would like to meet. It is high time I knew my goddaughter, and that you met my own daughter, whom I must shortly explain this to – I have been too much a coward to tell her anything. Your mothers were so close that I have every hope you two will be friends also.

Be on your guard until I arrive, and may the wind favour your flight.
Your absent yet doting godfather,
Capt. P. Sheridan
A.S. Spitfire

"Woah," was all she could say. "That would have changed things, huh."

"That was how your aunt got on the trail of the Spitfire Project," Mac explained. "So I suppose it wasn't entirely useless."

For the first time, Sola looked up at her aunt. She half expected the woman to scold her for being so rude as to kill a man, but there was no such reaction.

"You never had any chance of living a normal life, did you," Judith sighed. "I did try my hardest."

"Is that why you didn't tell me about any of this? A godfather who flew an airship? You going to Africa?"

"Aislin and Patrick dragged your parents into all sorts of scrapes," she said, glancing at Mac. "I suppose it's a family trait. But yes, I didn't want to put those adventurous thoughts into your head. Young girls have a tendency to think these things will be fun and romantic, rather than painful and unpleasant."

How true that was.

"It's had it's romantic moments," she replied, unable to break the habit of contradicting her aunt. "You didn't like Africa then?"

"It had its moments," replied Judith. 'However, it was also... I hated a lot of it."

"You shouldn't speak like this is over," Mac said.

"Isn't it?" Sola said. "I killed him."

The sentence sounded strange aloud, but again, there was none of the expected guilt.

"Edward Bingley," Mac replied. "He'll still be after us. And with that much power, I don't think I could spend my life running if I tried."

"What are we going to do, then?" Sola asked, frowning.

"You're going to come home with me," said Judith instantly.

Sola gave her a look of extreme disbelief.

"After the conversation we just had, do you really think so?"

"It might be for the best, Sola," Mac said softly.

"What?! Why?"

Judith and Mac exchanged a look, which infuriated her beyond belief.

"This is *about* me, I have been in this from the beginning, it's my life on the line too!"

"I telegrammed Bingley," Mac said. "He's back in London, so I asked him to come over for dinner on the Spitfire tonight. It's because your life is on the line that you should leave."

"What are you going to say?"

"I'm going to give him the file."

"You can't do that. Our parents died for it."

Mac rested her head in her hand.

"I know that. Of course I know that. But in the end, Sola, I just don't care. A small, light, fast aircraft? It would be amazing, sure, but I'd rather be alive, wouldn't you? Your parents may have died for the Spitfire Project, but Ethan died for you."

"So you're just going to give up."

"If it will save us, yes."

"Then I'm going to be here. I want to see him. I'll have dinner with you. Don't you dare try to tell me that I can't."

"Alright," said Mac.

It crossed Sola's mind for a second that the captain sounded even more defeated than she felt.

"I will not allow this," said Judith resolutely.

"I'm not asking for permission," Sola replied, equally firmly. "Do you not see how far beyond that I am now?"

The three women looked at each other across the table.

"I do. My god, you're so like your mother."

"Is that a compliment?"

It was meant to be a joke, it was meant to lighten the mood, but instead Judith seemed on the brink of tears.

"It means you're beautiful, and very brave, and you terrify me."

So quietly that Sola almost didn't notice, Mac stood and slipped out of the room, leaving her to stare at her aunt, the woman she'd lived with her whole life, and didn't recognise at all.

Mac must have said something, because nobody interrupted Judith and Sola in the lounge for the next two hours. They spoke like they should have done for Sola's whole life, giving up completely on the boundaries and walls that had existed between them. To Sola's horror and relief, the empty apathy that had taken control of her began to subside. The pain was raw again, bright and real, but that was the way it ought to be. She didn't cry, though she came close several times, and to her relief, neither did Judith. That much emotion perhaps would have been pushing the relationship too far. However by the time that Judith left, Sola had come to peace with the elements of her upbringing she had always resented her aunt for, not to mention *finally* heard some stories about her parents.

She went to return Mac's gun to her, pushing open the door as had become her custom. Sola stopped in her tracks.

The captain was sitting on her desk, with her legs wrapped around Marcus Tate as they embraced each other. To her relief, they were still fully clothed. She coughed loudly. The lovers sprung apart, Mac jumping off her desk immediately.

"Knocking, Austin, *seriously*," she said, going red.

Beside her Marcus laughed. She shoved him.

"Get out."

Sola felt bad as he began to comply.

"No, I just wanted to return your gun," she lifted it as though proving herself. "I'll just leave it..." she went to place it on the table.

"Marcus, give us a minute," Mac said, calming a little.

Sola didn't stop him this time, blushing as he passed her and stepped into the hall, closing the door behind him.

As soon as it shut, Mac laughed.

"Sorry you saw that," she said. "Though it was your fault."

"You didn't have to make him leave, really."

"Edward Bingley will be here in a few hours. It's probably a good idea that we speak, Sola. Also... you should keep that gun."

"I can use the one Tristan gave me. I picked it up from the workshop: Eth- he'd already adapted the grip."

Mac shook her head.

"That's the one my father made so it worked perfectly in his left hand. It's never worked right for me, so it makes sense you have it. Besides, apparently he was your godfather, and I can't think of anything else to give you as a keepsake."

"Oh... well, thanks."

"Speaking of giving you things," Mac continued, walking over to her drawers. "A belt, finished at long last."

She grabbed it and threw it over. Sola buckled it around her waist and slipped the gun into the holster.

"Is the transformation complete?" she asked, grinning.

"You don't look like the same girl," Mac answered.

"I'm not."

CHAPTER THIRTY-ONE

I feel as though the file is accusing me as it sits there. I have looked through it again and again – a few of the sketches make it clear what Father was planning to build, but I would have no idea how. Maybe if Ethan was here... but he's not, and that doesn't bear thinking about. I need to do this. Father made me promise to save Sola Austin: he didn't mention this project. It would mean nothing to him, in comparison, I am sure of that. This is everything I have been trying to tell myself, but there is still the guilt. Sola doesn't help the situation, with her accusing glances (hers actually are accusing, it's not my own conscience troubling me).

Even Marcus cannot keep my mind off Edward Bingley's visit tonight: I keep seeing his smile as he handed me that glass of champagne, and wondering what I am thinking of, to invite the man who tried to kill me around for a second chance.

Mac looked across at the Spitfire Project file, and shook her head. She'd tried to think of any way out of this situation, and was still hoping for a last minute stroke of genius, a fully formed idea that would appear in her mind.

She picked up the file again, and then put it back down. Shoving her chair out, she stood up violently and began to pace around the study. Then it came to her. She sat down and began to write.

When she was done, she stepped out onto the back balcony, to see that Sola was already there.

"Aren't you going to put on a dress for our esteemed guest?" she teased, on seeing that the other woman was still in trousers and a shirt, with her belt and the gun at her side, and her hair scraped back.

"Not a chance," Sola said seriously. "I want him to be scared of me."

"I think the chances of that are a little low, don't you?"

"I think they're quite high actually."

Mac looked at her in surprise, unable to detect any sarcasm.

"Oh?"

"My parents are dead because of him. Ethan is dead, not because of him, but it's keeping me angry. He poisoned you. I killed a man this morning – a man I've known my whole life, mind... and even if that weren't enough to scare him, people are always scared when you defy their expectations."

Her steely confidence restored a little of Mac's own faith.

"I'm glad you decided to stay for tonight," she said.

Sola glanced over and smiled.

"I have to see this through now, don't I?"

"I suppose that's one way to look at it."

"We should probably go up onto deck."

Mac gripped the chain of the compass and pulled it out from underneath her shirt. She flipped it open and glanced inside, then closed it, and allowed it to rest outside of her clothes for once.

"Yes, let's," she agreed.

The entire crew was up there. They had grudgingly agreed to make themselves absent while Bingley was aboard, for their own protection.

"We don't mind staying, Cap" James tried again. "Seriously, I've spent enough time off the Spitfire recently."

"This is only going to be for an hour or two, Riddle."

"You hope," interjected Tristan.

"You aren't suggesting I would let Bingley get the better of me twice, are you?" she replied, forcing a jovial tone. "Go. Eat some decent food in the city. Try not to worry yourselves to death, and we'll see you back here in a few hours."

"This is getting longer and longer," Rob pointed out.

"Oh for god's sake, must you three be so picky? Your loyalty is touching, but I expect this shall be a battle of minds rather than muscle."

"Why do you think they're so worried," she heard Marcus behind her.

She'd planned on objecting to his attempt at a joke, but the obvious concern in his eyes hit her like a brick wall. She reached out a hand, which he grasped tightly.

"When I said 'be careful', this wasn't what I had in mind," he said.

Mac threw her arms around his neck and hugged him hard. Resting her forehead against his, she tried to force out words that she knew she should say, that she'd never been able to.

"You know that I..." she faltered.

"Yes," he said. "And you know that I do too."

"I know."

"Good."

She kissed him quickly, not caring that they were in front of the crew.

"Oh, so she doesn't get mocked," she heard Sola snidely remark.

"Go on," she said, pulling away. "I'll see you soon, I promise."

"Be careful."

"I always am," she replied, to which he just laughed.

One by one the men reluctantly descended onto the docks, as a carriage pulled up outside. Edward Bingley stepped out and walked up the ramp onto the deck. Seeing him again was strange, knowing everything that she had discovered.

"Mr Bingley," she said, and swallowed, trying not to let her nerves show. "Good evening."

"Good evening, Captain Sheridan," he replied, sounding far more composed. "And Lady Austin I assume, although you look very different these days."

"You two have met?" said Mac, surprised.

"Oh, encountered each other at balls and other such functions."

"You'll forgive me if I don't remember you," said Sola. Mac was impressed by her cold, steady voice. "Such tedious affairs tend to involve many lengthy introductions."

"I completely sympathise," he smiled. "Is there a reason your crew have left, Captain Sheridan?"

"They aren't a part of this. I'd hate for any more of them to be hurt."

"I'm sorry any of them have been hurt. What happened?"

She stared at him in disbelief.

"Well, one was manipulated into betraying his own friends, and has been left unemployed, unable to support his family, and wallowing in self-pity and guilt, I would expect. That was your doing, if I'm not mistaken," she said.

"Ah. Mr Large."

She was glad that he didn't deny it.

"I didn't *make* him do anything. Nor I did make you fire him, though I understand your decision to do so."

"Another was burnt to death," she continued, trying to sound matter-of-fact. "Not your fault, to be fair, although I believe you gave Duke Bernard his first taste of fire starting."

"Of course, Russell is how you have connected the dots. Pathetic man, really. Where is he now?"

"Austin shot him," Mac said. "We dropped him off at the mortuary."

For the first time, Bingley looked a little ruffled.

"Well, Lady Austin, you've done this country a service at least."

"More than I can say for you," Sola replied.

"We should discuss this below deck, really," Mac interjected.

"Quite."

She led him through to the crew lounge, keeping away from her study, where the report was still sitting on her desk.

"You'll forgive me, we don't have a formal dining area," she said as she walked over to the drinks cabinet. "Are you a whiskey or a Scotch man?"

"Scotch, please," he said, sitting at their cards table and crossing his legs.

"Whiskey for you, Sola?"

"Indeed," Sola replied, not taking her eyes off Bingley as she sat across from him. Mac took over their drinks, then made another for herself and joined them.

"So you want to know what happened?" Bingley asked.

"I think we already know. You were afraid that this machine our parents were creating would put you out of business, so you blackmailed

Duke Bernard into destroying it."

"That's a little simplistic. First I tried to buy them out, but they were incorruptible apparently. Except Russell – he was the government liaison to the project – had a family. His son was his weak link, yes, I exploited it. I had him withdraw funding from the project, tell the government it was a pipe dream, never going to work, that sort of thing."

"Then my father started funding it himself," said Sola.

"Exactly. I already had the perfect means of controlling Russell, so it seemed foolish to involve anyone else."

"Did you have him kill my mother too?" she asked.

Bingley laughed.

"Once George Austin died in the blaze, I didn't have to *make* Russell do anything. He'd do it just to protect himself. Very handy, actually."

A shiver ran down Mac's spine.

"How can you be so cold?" she asked, not caring how pathetic it sounded. "How can you not care that these are people's lives?"

"If you want to be successful in this world, you have to accept it for what it is," Bingley said. "You can't just pretend that only the good parts exist. God, child, I have nothing against *you*, do you think I wanted to hurt you, do you think I'm some sort of monster?"

"That is the impression I am getting, yes. And please, Mr Bingley, do not refer to me as a child. I am certainly no longer one, and that is largely due to you."

He inclined his head and sipped his drink.

"You didn't bring me here to accuse me of stealing your youth, *Captain*, did you?"

"No, Mr Bingley I didn't. Nor to accuse you of murder, attempted murder, blackmail, drug smuggling, or many of your other crimes. I asked you here because *all* I want is a peaceful life. I don't want to be looking over my shoulder. I want to run my ship, and my business. I want to go abroad, and not because I'm afraid I'll be murdered in my sleep if I stay here. So what will it take?"

"I assume you have something in mind."

She looked at him for a few seconds, wondering if it was wise to reveal her whole hand so soon, but he hadn't left her with much of a choice.

"I have the file. The Spitfire Project. All my father's calculations and designs. You can have it. Destroy it, end it for good."

"Destroy it?" Bingley laughed. "Why would I do that?"

Mac frowned.

"Isn't that what this whole thing has been about? Not wanting these aircraft to exist?"

"I thought you ran a business, Captain. It's been about not wanting somebody else to *own* them. If I'd known Russell had the file the whole time..."

"Well, in that case, wait here and I'll just fetch it."

She could feel Sola staring at her in horror, and determinedly did not meet her gaze. Doing her best not to run, she left and went along to her study. She grabbed the file and a matchbox from her desk and walked briskly back to the lounge.

"There you go, all yours," she said, rudely shoving the papers into his hands.

"Thank you, Captain Sheridan, I must say I expected more of an argument."

"I bet you did, you bastard," she replied, and struck a match, dropping it on top of the file.

He shook it off, but the paper had already lit. He blew desperately on the flames, but it made no difference, soon the fire had reached his hands and he dropped the file onto the table. The three of them could do nothing but watch as the fire burnt out, leaving ashes and a black mark on the varnish.

"That was reckless, Captain," said Bingley, trying to regain his calm.

She picked her glass up from the table, distastefully regarding the ashes floating on the surface before drinking anyway.

"Yes, it's more my style than measured and contained."

"What is protecting you now?"

She shrugged.

"What's not? You have no reason to kill me, do you? That was it, it's gone. The only reason I didn't destroy it before is that you wouldn't have believed I did. See, you're a *businessman*. You don't kill for revenge.

It's not personal. It's just what's necessary. Isn't that right?"

"Yes, it is."

"It is no longer necessary."

"You could tell people about this, I can't allow that to happen."

Mac laughed.

"Who would believe us? And who would act on it if we did? You are impervious to legal action, it's disgusting, but for once it's benefiting somebody else as well. Please leave my ship, Mr Bingley."

"You've copied it."

"I'm sorry?"

"That was your father's work, you wouldn't just burn it."

"I assure you I *would*, Father's inventing meant very little to me."

But there was something about his face that told her he wouldn't be reasoned with.

"Where is your study?" he said, standing.

Mac laughed.

"Follow me," she said. "I honestly didn't realise it meant so much to you, I might have asked for more than a peaceful life."

"I can give you money," he said. "If you give it to me now rather than making me search."

"That really was the only copy," she said. "Feel free to search to your heart's content."

She took him to her study, where he looked through the bookshelves, and her desk and drawers, leaving everything in a mess on the floor. Mac kept silent, fighting an urge to laugh. He kept his calm demeanor as best he could, slowly going about his search, but she could tell he was becoming frantic. It was scary, yet still entertaining, to watch him lose just a little of his control.

"Was that really the only copy?" Sola whispered to her.

She just smiled.

When he was done with her study, Bingley swung around and snapped,

"Where did your father work? Are his notes still there?"

"Who knows? Ethan may have cleared them out, I didn't."

"Take me there."

"Manners, Mr Bingley."

"I am not *playing*, child."

She bristled at the word, but said nothing.

"Sola, lead the way to the workshop."

Giving her a look of concern, Sola turned and began to walk. She didn't want to let Bingley into her father's workplace, and she imagined Sola felt the same way about letting him into Ethan's. However she felt the best thing was to allow him to exhaust his search and hopefully leave. It wasn't the peaceful agreement she'd originally aimed for, but then she thought of how much she'd hate herself for making a deal with him.

They stepped inside, and she felt a pang of sorrow at how virtually everything remained untouched, as though Ethan were going to appear around the corner and say, 'careful, don't touch that'.

Thinking of that, Mac said, "Be careful what you touch," as Bingley reached out toward a workbench with chemicals across it.

Defiantly, he grabbed a vial. Mac shoved Sola backwards and launched herself toward him, but she was too late. Everything exploded.

CHAPTER THIRTY-TWO

The doctor says she will live, but I somehow won't believe it until I see her move again. So still, with bandages draped over all her burns, she does look dead. The repairs on the Spitfire are coming along steadily – I just hope Mac will be able to fly when her ship is.

I was terrified that the crew would be angry with me for not preventing it somehow, but I should have known that was foolish. It feels strange to have these people so genuinely happy that I am mostly unharmed (my hearing returned after a few hours, thank god). I know for sure that I will never leave them now, no matter what happens to Mac. But it wouldn't be the same without her.

Sola looked up as she saw movement in the corner of her eye. She stared at Mac, but seeing nothing, sighed. She was about to put pen to paper, but saw Mac's eyes flicker again.

"Mac? Mac are you awake?"

The eyelids flicked open and shut a few more times before remaining open.

"I can't believe I let him into the workshop," she croaked. "Should have seen that coming."

"It was a bit stupid," Sola said, tears springing to her eyes as she began to laugh.

Mac laughed with her, then stopped.

"Ouch. My face got burnt, huh?"

"Yes. Not too badly, it should sort itself. You have a few other burns too. I'm afraid your arm-"

Mac looked down at the limb, and choked. A metal contraption had replaced her flesh-and-blood arm, the nerves damaged beyond repair. Tentatively, she lifted one mechanical finger and then the next, and then finally the whole thing.

"This is fucking weird."

"The doctors said it would take time to reach full dexterity, but with hard work it should be possible," Sola hurried to say.

"I can't afford this," Mac said. "I mean, seriously, I'd be in debt for the rest of my life."

"Well, evidently my family being wealthy isn't the worst thing in the world," Sola said.

"I can't accept this from you..."

"It's not actually from me," she said.

"It's from me," came a voice from the doorway. "Nice to see you awake, Captain Sheridan."

Sola grinned at her aunt.

"Well, Lady Austin, thank you very much but..."

"Oh accept it, girl. I owe you my niece's life, after all."

She said it so harshly that it didn't sound sentimental in the slightest, and Sola laughed.

"She won't take no for an answer, Mac."

Mac shook her head, and pushed back her hair with her good hand. Judith came into the room, followed by her maidservant. Sola smiled at Grace, who'd been incredibly relieved to see her safe and well.

"What happened to Bingley?"

"Dead," Sola said shortly.

Mac sank back into her pillow with an audible sigh of relief.

"It's over?" she asked, cautiously hopeful.

"It is over," Sola confirmed.

"I don't believe it. The Spitfire?"

"In the process of repairs. I did pay for that."

"Sola... I would have..."

"I know you could have afforded it, though not easily," Sola said, "but it felt like something I could do. That said, you are short a few crew members, and you're going to have to relearn how to use your arm."

"Thanks for reminding me, Austin," she groaned.

"Well, I was just thinking, I could probably help out. A bit longer.

Or a lot longer. If you wanted."

"Lady Austin, are you saying you'd like to be on the payroll?" Mac asked. "Long-term? You want to join the crew?"

"Well... if you'll have me."

To her dismay, Mac looked over at Judith.

"*If* Sola were asking your permission," she said, "would you give it?"

Her aunt stared hardly at the wounded captain.

"Reluctantly," she said. "But I don't think she is asking me."

"I was asking you," Mac said. "I'll look after her."

"I want her to have her own cabin," Judith said.

"I wouldn't take her out of the one she's in," Mac replied. "It was mine, but I expect I'd sleep in the study most nights even if it were empty."

Judith nodded and stretched out a hand. Slowly, painstakingly, Mac brought her metal and clockwork replacement up to shake it. Sola could see she didn't bend the fingers, and wondered how long it would take for her to become comfortable with the replacement.

"Is that a yes, Captain?" Sola asked.

"Yes, Austin," Mac grinned. "I'd be happy to have you."

Sola grinned back at her.

"I think Marcus is waiting outside," she said. "I'll go fetch him. They'll only let him in if they think..."

"He's your servant," Mac replied.

Sola was glad she hadn't said 'slave'.

"Exactly."

"Go get him. I expect he's been a nightmare."

It was true, the man had been worried and pacing and yelling at the hospital staff when they refused to let him in. Sola had brought him inside a few times, but then he found the sight of Mac unconscious too disturbing to handle. She found him outside the doors, staring at the building.

"Come on in, she's awake."

He stared at her in shock, and then was by her side immediately, practically running through the corridors, forcing Sola to keep up so people could see she was with him. But when he burst through the door, it wasn't Mac he stared at. Grace stared straight back at him, and it was obvious something was going on that the rest of them weren't privy to.

"Brother?" Grace said, her voice hitching.

Sola looked at Mac, who had her living hand to her mouth, lips parted, eyes wide.

"Sister," Marcus replied, and walked up to her. He put his hand on her cheek. "Is it really you?"

In a blink, the two of them were hugging tightly, as though they were glued together.

"I've been looking so long," Marcus was whispering into her ear, still clearly audible to the rest of the room.

"What happened to you? Are you free?"

"Yes, yes, I'm free. The Austins own you?" he asked, glancing over at Sola.

"She's free to leave," Judith said.

"I wouldn't want to," insisted Grace, pulling out of the embrace. "They treat me well, brother, I've been paid for years now."

"Are you sure? Because I can look after you, if you wanted..."

"I'm just glad to find you, I'd given up hope," she said, smiling broadly. "But I will stay with Lady Austin."

"Thank you, Grace," said Judith, and Sola could hear that she was being perfectly genuine.

"I can't deal with any more revelations," Mac said, rolling her eyes.

Marcus laughed and turned to her. The laughter died on his lips when he saw her arm, and the bandages across her body. He crouched by her side and stroked her hair.

"How do you feel?"

"Hurts like fuck," she said. "Can't feel my arm. Don't *have* an arm. Alive though, and going to be just fine apparently."

"I shouldn't have left."

"I'm glad you did," she said firmly. "You have the file?"

"Of course I do."

"You *did* make a copy," Sola exclaimed. "Why didn't you tell me?!"

"I figured it was safer if less people knew," she said, grinning. "I did make a copy, though it still means virtually nothing to me. I figure if I'm lucky enough to stumble across another inventing prodigy, they can have it. It seemed like a lot of hard work to just burn."

"You mean you planned the whole thing?"

Mac laughed.

"I left room for improvisation," she said. "It took some unexpected twists."

"No kidding," Sola grumbled, but couldn't help smiling, which ruined the effect.

It was a few weeks before Mac was ready to leave hospital. In some ways this was useful – it gave them time to get the Spitfire into working order, for Sola to spend some more time with Judith, for Mac to spend some more time with Marcus, who was also doing a lifetime of catching up with Grace. The crew followed Mac's instructions, setting up a contract to carry a batch of tealeaves from London to Rome when they set sail again, and hiring two extra men for the trip. None of them had ever been to Italy, and Sola soon became eager to take to the skies again. Mac had it worse, being stuck in the same building day-in, day-out, and was thrilled when she was at last discharged.

Even having been unconscious at the time, Sola could see the differences between this and the last time they departed London. Marcus, Judith and Grace were all there to see the Spitfire off from the docks, in broad daylight. Marcus and Mac had a whispered conversation before they boarded, and she was looking forward to weaseling out the details from Mac over whiskey and a card game later that evening.

Now, the captain was grinning broadly at the wheel, clearly loving having her ship in her hands once again. Tristan was swinging from the ropes, racing the new crewmembers and outpacing them with ease. Mac had asked him to be first mate, which he of course accepted, though Sola didn't see that his duties had changed at all. Sitting on the steps she watched Vertigo flutter around her head a few times, then cracked open her journal and wrote.

To be on board the Spitfire for no reason other than my wanting it gives a wonderful feeling of freedom. Never in my life would I have expected to end up in this position, yet I know now that it is perfect. I don't know if I would have ended up with the anarchists or the aristocrats in another life, but I can't help feeling neither would have been the same as this. One cannot easily change one's fate, but not everyone's fate is right for them. Mine certainly wasn't.

"Oi, Austin!" Mac yelled from the wheel.

"Yes, Captain?"

"I'm paying you now, come and do some bloody work!"

Sola laughed and closed the journal, leaving it on the steps as she ran up to get instructions from her captain and closest friend.

ACKNOWLEDGMENTS

& you, by the way

Thank you to all my friends and family - I couldn't function without. you.

Thanks also to Mrs Stevenson who encouraged me when I was seven years old, and Mr Cotter who later fanned the flames of my love of English, I wouldn't still be writing if not for you both.

And a massive thank you to everyone who makes NaNoWriMo a possibility. I didn't believe I could write a novel in a month, and you proved me completely wrong.

ABOUT THE AUTHOR

Hayley McLennan has been writing for as long as she can remember. The Spitfire Project is not her first novel, but it is the first one she's liked enough to bother publishing.

She... *I* (why bother pretending someone else is writing this?) am also a fanfiction writer, and if you read my fics then I apologise for how long it's been since I updated (this will be valid no matter when you read it).

Made in the USA
Charleston, SC
16 February 2013